# Mint & Other Stories

Grateful acknowledgement to *Cyphers*, where most of these stories were first published.

# MINT
## & OTHER STORIES

Adrian Kenny

THE LILLIPUT PRESS
DUBLIN

First published 2025 by
THE LILLIPUT PRESS

62–63 Sitric Road,
Arbour Hill,
Dublin 7,
Ireland
www.lilliputpress.ie

Copyright © Adrian Kenny, 2025

10 9 8 7 6 5 4 3 2 1

All rights reserved. No part of this publication may be reproduced in any form or by any means without the prior permission of the publisher.

Stories from this collection first appeared in *Cyphers*

A CIP record for this title is available from The British Library.

Paperback ISBN 978 1 84351 956 0

Set in 11.5 pt on 16 pt Sabon LT Std by Compuscript
Printed and bound in Ireland by Sprint Books, Dublin

*To Maurice Sheehan*

# CONTENTS

| | |
|---|---|
| Mint | 1 |
| Good Friday | 10 |
| English Pastoral | 19 |
| Weekends in Deptford | 38 |
| An Evening Prowl | 52 |
| Brothers | 77 |
| The Bathing Place | 92 |
| The Graveyard | 104 |
| A Fairy Tale | 115 |
| Mister Pock – Finale | 135 |
| Two Cousins | 148 |

# MINT

How will my house be remembered? As the one where mint grew out through the front garden railings? People pluck leaves as they pass and rub them between their fingers.

A bunch of fresh mint wrapped in damp newspaper with Arabic print: that was Fatima's gift to me the evening she arrived. Crumbs of brown clay clung to the roots. Her sister said, 'This is for your help with the immigration forms.' Fatima stood silent in a black shawl. I thought, My grandmother must have looked like that when she arrived as a girl in New York.

Her sister was married and lived up the street. Fatima minded the children to earn her keep. She was pale, thin and hard-faced, with large dark eyes that gave her a staring look. Everything was new to her. She thought the black-and-gold bin at the corner was a post box. When I told her what *Litter* meant, she smiled. In a few months her face filled out. We used to chat whenever we met. She was learning English, and spoke a little French much better than mine.

One day she asked me to help her find a part-time job – she wanted a change from minding children. I asked a neighbour if she needed help with housework, and I asked in the restaurant. But her sister wanted her at home. They had an argument in front of me another day. Fatima cried and said she was *'une esclave'*. She wanted 'liberté'. She wanted 'la vie'. The next time we met she wanted 'un homme' to share 'la vie'.

That was in July, when the sister and husband went back to Morocco for a family wedding. They planned to leave the children behind with Fatima, but at the last minute the children won and went with their parents. Fatima was left to mind the house.

I was in my front garden a few days later when I noticed a glamorous young woman in a red miniskirt, with a red velvet band on long black hair, coming up the street. It was Fatima. She stood to talk. I had planted the mint she had given me, and it had taken root. She reached through the railings and plucked a few leaves, then invited me to her house for tea.

When I called she was in the back yard, kneeling before a mirror, putting henna in her hair. She was barefoot, at home in the sun, her skirt turned up to her thighs. Beata, an old woman who had minded the children before Fatima arrived, was also there. She was a Czech refugee, sad and gentle, who used to whisper to our dog and give it crusts of bread she kept in her handbag. Now her job was chaperoning Fatima – not from me: I was married and middle-aged, of no concern, but of use maybe.

While Fatima made mint tea she told me how I could help. She wanted to find a man. With a husband she could leave her sister's house and have a life of her own. She had only a month to do it, for when her sister returned she would be tied again to the children. There was someone at home who was interested. He wanted to ring her, but she had no phone. Could she give him my number to call? I agreed.

For several nights after that our phone would ring, a man would say, '*Fatima, s'il vous plait?*' then I would walk up to Fatima, she would run down, and for ten or fifteen minutes our hall was filled with laughter and love-whisperings in Arabic. To give her privacy, my wife turned up the TV.

It was a fine summer. She must have thought all our summers were like that. In the evenings she used to sit at the open front door on a chair set backwards, leaning over its rail, while old Beata dozed inside. I was walking our dog round the block when she invited me again for tea. I went down to my garden, plucked a few more leaves and brought them up to her house. A tape was playing, there was a basin of millet and a sieve on the floor, a scent of charcoal smoke. She swayed to the music, singing the words, '*Je suis seule comme un arbre ...*'

Over tea she told me the latest. She had gone down one night to the phone box at Kelly's Corner and rung her boyfriend in Morocco. She called him 'Numero un'.

I said, 'Good.'

She shook her head. It was too slow, remote, and besides he hadn't a visa. But as she had left the phone box a man had smiled at her, then offered to walk her home. By the time they reached her door he had made a date.

'Did you go?'

She looked across the hall to the sitting room, then nodded.

'What happened?'

'Everything!' She clapped her hands and laughed, waking old Beata, who hurried in. He was a doctor, and a Moslem – her face was serious again – so they had a lot to talk about. But it didn't mean anything. He was engaged – he had a fiancée in Pakistan. She still needed my help.

She wanted to marry; she had to. A single woman couldn't live on her own, and anyhow she couldn't afford a flat. Over other cups of tea that month I heard of her attempts. She went for walks in St Stephen's Green, carrying a camera, pretending she was a tourist, asking men to take her photo, then chatting them up. One man gave her his phone number, but nothing came of it. Time was passing, soon her sister would be back, and Fatima would be at home again with the children. She wanted to live, her life was going – she tilted the tea pot to show me the green sodden mint leaves at the bottom – 'like that'.

She seemed to lose spirit that last week of her freedom. She stopped sitting in the evening at her door. One day I saw her drifting past my house. I should have known better. There was no room for drifting in her life. The day before her sister returned, Fatima disappeared.

Her sister was shocked, worried for Fatima's safety, but more worried by losing her childminder. She was an ambitious practical woman, busy shouldering her family into prosperity. I was used to seeing her car drive past, with a new carpet, a TV satellite dish or a china cabinet in the back seat. Now her children were piled in the back seat, and her face had a frown as she searched the streets. She called to our house at eight o'clock one morning, and another night at ten, hoping to catch Fatima there. But I had no more idea than she where Fatima was.

Our phone rang one evening and the plaintive, faint voice from Morocco said, '*Fatima, s'il vous plait?*' I said she wasn't at home. He clicked his tongue and hung up.

A few days later, the phone rang again. It was Fatima.

'Are you all right?' I said. 'Where are you?'

'I'm with Beata. I'm OK. I met someone.'

'How?'

'La chance!' She laughed like a girl. She had met a young man in the refugee office. His name was Kamal. They were getting married. She needed my help. She brought him to visit that night when it was dark.

He was a serious, balding, not-so-young man with a bewildered look, as if things were going too fast. They were getting married next week, she said. Her sister and brother-in-law refused to attend. Would I drive her to the mosque? Kamal wiped his forehead and asked if he could use the bathroom. While he was gone Fatima asked in a whisper if there had been any phone call from Numero un? I nodded. She pressed a finger to her lips as Kamal returned.

She wore a long cream dress on her wedding day. She looked the part. She was the pianist who knew the music by heart. Three young men passed as she was getting out of the car, and at once she got back inside, drawing her veil down over her eyes. The women sat apart from the men at the ceremony, and afterwards at the wedding meal. I sat with a Tunisian boy who stopped eating, raised a finger and smiled each time an *Ul-lu-lu* cry came across the corridor from the women's room. As I was leaving I met Kamal walking up and down the mosque yard, smoking a cigarette. When I congratulated him he nodded and, as if repeating some wise old Arab proverb, said, 'It completes something.'

The mint spread in my front garden. A neighbour admired it and asked for a slip. When I set a slip in my back garden, it sent up green leaves the following spring, and then in August the pale purple flowers appeared. It must have been a year before I saw Fatima again.

It was one of those grey winter Sunday afternoons when everybody was inside, when Dublin seemed a place where man was never meant to live. A seagull glided between the bare trees. The low sky strained, as if trying to rain, then the clouds lightened for a minute, as if the sun might crawl through, then the greyness thickened again. I had to get out.

Going down the street I saw Kamal coming up, and Fatima pushing a go-cart behind. They'd had a baby but didn't speak of that, though they interrupted each other in their eagerness to talk. She yawned as he discussed democracy in Morocco. When I complained about the weather, Kamal shrugged. 'It won't do you any harm.'

'You sound like an Irishman,' I said.

'I am an Irishman,' he said. He had Irish citizenship now, and a job in a cardboard box factory in Tallaght. Fatima rolled her large dark eyes.

'He's not my sort of man,' she said, when I met her next. She was alone with their baby son, who was already starting to walk. She looked thin again. She said she had pains all the time. It was the weather. When the child cried, she slapped him hard on the face.

The weather suited the mint, and it spread. I was thinning it one day when Fatima called and told me the news. She and Kamal had divorced. Their son was going to a playschool. A boy had snatched old Beata's handbag, dragged her along the pavement when she wouldn't let go her precious crusts; she had died in hospital. Then Fatima came to the point: she was applying for Irish citizenship, and wanted my help with the forms.

The mint died every winter, the frost burned it black, but by now I knew that the roots were alive and fresh leaves would return in the spring. I was walking by the canal one evening, looking at a clutch of ducklings that had just hatched – little brown balls of down darting through the reeds, running onto the lily pads, pecking at flies. A serious voice behind me said, 'Hello.' It was Kamal.

He was sitting on a bench with a woman, sharing a bag of sunflower seeds. She came from Ukraine, he said, but had worked in Istanbul for several years. When I asked what her job had been, she looked down. The red varnish on her fingernails was chipped. She hadn't good English, he explained. He said Fatima was living in Parnell Street with another man.

I was in the front garden when she passed by the other day. She looked old and tired. She was pregnant again, and leaned against the railings to rest as we talked. Her son was with his father. She was going to see her sister. She had Irish citizenship at last. She looked at the green mint, growing luxuriant, three feet high, and gave her sad, hard smile and said, 'Oh. *La nature.*'

# GOOD FRIDAY

Around the quarter everyone's wife seemed to have lost interest in sex. That was the talk in the pub. Mick said she said it was her back. Roddy said she said it didn't do anything for her now. He said he said, 'What's this? What do I do?' He said she said, 'Do what you like but don't be telling me.'

Mick said he missed the time when they used to sit up watching the late-night film, even if it was boring, all the more if it was boring, building up the pleasure of going to bed. And then it all stopped; the tap was turned off.

Roddy said he had smiled at a girl in the bus. She had stood up and offered him her seat.

Mick said, 'Ah well, we've served our purpose. Nature doesn't need us anymore.'

Roddy said, 'Well I need nature.'

He said there was a woman he had gone out with as a student, and met sometimes for coffee when she was back in town. The last time they met she complained about her husband. He asked would she like to go away some weekend, and she agreed.

They planned it carefully. She was coming over at Easter to visit her mother, who was in a home. He was going fishing to Galway, where they could meet. His office closed on Thursday, he went down that evening, found a hotel and booked a room. 'A double,' – he looked at the ceiling – 'the other half's coming tomorrow.'

The receptionist was indifferent to his private life. She looked at a computer screen. 'We have a single for tonight, and tomorrow there'll be a double free.' She gave him a form that took five minutes to fill.

The night they had first slept together, he had written Mr and Mrs in the register. It was that long ago, another time. He had chosen the hotel, the only one he could think of, where his parents had once gone on holiday. It had ended there; in fact it had never begun. They had been shy and innocent. She had cried when, ashamed, he had gone downstairs to the bar. But that night had brought them together in another way: it was from there they had each set out into the world.

He went for a walk after dinner, exploring the small city streets: he hadn't been there for years. He had forgotten the blue-grey limestone, the bridges, the sense of water everywhere, the sound of Irish – '*Ól suas é, is fada ó chonaigh mé thú*' – an old woman's voice in a bar. It was strange, and it was home. It was like an image of his life, and of hers. Rooted in different countries, they had no intention of uprooting now; they were meeting for a weekend, no more. Standing on a bridge, watching the river flood down to the sea, he remembered his pretext and rang his wife. Three days of fishing, he said, and he'd be back, refreshed. She laughed and said she'd be refreshed as well, sleeping without his snoring.

He had forgotten too the pleasure of sleeping alone: spreading his arms and legs like a starfish across the bed; getting up in the night – he had reached that age – looking out the window and seeing how the stars had moved; lying down again, thinking, Into the arms of Lethe and trying to remember as he drifted back to sleep who or what Lethe was. He wasn't anxious or guilty. Their pleasure would simply make good that innocent, unhappy night long ago.

## Good Friday

Her skin was still soft, without make-up, and her fine hair was a beautiful grey. He kissed her lips when she stepped from the train. She smiled and put her tongue in his mouth. Their room wasn't ready; the receptionist took her suitcase, then they went out into the morning sun. The streets were empty, everywhere was closed – the shops and pubs, the small museum – for Good Friday.

He had come by car, and they drove out along the coast, where already the weather was changing. Silvery walls of mist were moving in from the sea. They walked down by a stream clotted with brown foam, among sheep sheltering in hollows worn into the slope, down to where green waves washed over black decks of rock. She stood and held her arms open to the spray, the wild elements, but it seemed to him a youthful gesture that was not natural. As if she sensed his thought she fell behind, picking strands of sheep wool from the heather.

It was easier back in the car, in the warmth of the heater. Wiping the steamed windscreen, smoothing the sheep wool on her lap, she talked as they drove further. Her husband had a girlfriend now, a neighbour he visited every weekend on his bicycle. He said you didn't stop doing something you liked just because someone else didn't like it – he had that sort of blunt English honesty. But otherwise he was a good husband, and there was the house to think of, and the children. She would stay with him, though she missed the warmth of someone close, nothing fixed, nothing special, somebody you could turn to now and then. He reached across and touched her cheek.

They came to a village, another empty street, the pub and the shop both closed; but as she wiped the windscreen again she looked out. She remembered this place: she had been here as a girl; her grandfather had come from these parts. She talked of him as they crossed the flat bogland towards the mountains that changed shade under high, sailing clouds. He had been a shopkeeper, undertaker, emigration agent, farmer – a sort of gombeen man. When the Troubles came, he had sold up and retired with his money to a safer part of the country. She told it with the plain humour of someone worn by life.

The land grew wilder, the bare beauty broken by squares of forestry, a large factory that looked abandoned. Cars pulled out of farm bungalow gates and passed at speed, their suspension sinking, rising with the uneven road; and five or ten miles on they saw the same cars parked outside other bungalows. As they reached a headland the sun came through and they saw a beach below light up slowly. By the time he had driven down a steep winding track, the dark wet sand had dried as bright as gold dust.

## Good Friday

When she stepped from the car, the strands of sheep wool fell from her lap but she didn't notice; she was looking about, smiling. He thought she was going to run down the beach and wade into the sea, her arms outspread again to the elements. But she was looking at a small graveyard enclosed by a stone wall a few yards up from the shore.

Her grandfather's sister was buried there, she said. She had a vague memory of coming here as a girl; or maybe she had simply been told of this place, and imagined the visit. They were at ease together now, looking for the gate, not finding it and laughing as they climbed over ivy that bushed wild on top of the wall. Inside was so overgrown that only the tops of the headstones showed, but crushing down briars and bracken they waded from grave to grave, peeling moss from the slabs, rubbing in grass to bring out faded lettering. Her legs were scratched, their faces bright with sweat – now the sun was warm; but they called to each other, urging each other on, and continued searching. Just as they were about to give up, he found it.

She stood beside him, looking down at the name cut in a flat tombstone whitened by time and weather. He heard skylarks singing, the sea falling on the shore as he was silent with her. He thought of that body vanished into the sandy earth they were standing on, and that this woman with the same name would be sleeping with him that night. Again, as if she read his thought, she asked if he believed in another life. He said there might be, in some way – as the bracken grew from the sandy earth. But dead was dead, she said; alive and dead were different. But imagine, he said, if it was more like a spectrum or like sound waves; with the colours and sounds we could see and hear extending into something finer. Imagine if life and death were both part of something far greater?

Silent again she looked for some souvenir to take, a flower or even a pebble, but there were only the briars and bracken. The grave was enclosed by a high kerb, with a small stone urn set at each corner. Seeing one had come loose and hung sideways on a rusted iron spike, he drew it free and gave it to her. They felt together again, laughing as he helped her up over the ivied wall, pressing his hand to her bottom. She linked his arm as they walked along the strand by the rippling foam line, talking.

The sun went in as suddenly as it had come out, the rain came down again and the gold sand darkened as if a shadow had passed over. When they reached the car it was pouring. They had gone further than they thought, he was tired and hungry now, and their talk faded like the daylight.

He concentrated on the black wet road, she passed the time picking scabs of lichen from the stone urn. When she held it up and asked what sort of stone it was, he said abruptly that he couldn't see in the dark, and she was silent.

They brought their cases to the new double room, then went downstairs for dinner. The bar was closed, of course, because it was Good Friday; but so was the dining room beside it. The receptionist drew close and confided that they could be served a meal in the Atlantic Suite. Following signs on the walls, they walked fifty yards of corridor that grew shabby as they reached the end, where they saw a door at the top of a short stairway.

When he opened the door the noise of music hit his ears. They stared into the function room. A middle-aged man with a glossy brown toupee, a gold chain on his wrist, was playing an electric keyboard. Scores of men and women sat drinking at small tables. A waitress serving at a makeshift bar smiled when he asked for dinner. When it came at last it was terrible: slabs of red gammon heaped with tinned sweetcorn, blinding yellow. The music was as bad, jazzed-up Irish ballads, but the crowd sang fiercely, their faces flushed, holding hands and swaying from side to side at each chorus. He said it was grotesque, grown men and women hiding in a hotel back room on Good Friday. She disagreed, she said it was great, an assertion of life against dying. He was so depressed now that he couldn't argue.

When they went up to their room and turned on the light, he saw the stone urn on the dressing table. Playing for time, he took it in his hands and said it looked like sandstone, but he wasn't certain. By then she was in bed, smiling. As he undressed he heard an engine throb outside the window: their room was at the back, above some sort of generator. He turned off the light and slipped grimly into bed beside her.

It was just as it had been that night long ago. But now she didn't cry, and he didn't go down to the bar. He said that he was tired; she said that she was tired too, beautifully tired; it didn't matter. They lay side by side, talking of the sun turning the sand to gold, the rain turning it dark again, the larks singing, the scent of crushed bracken in the graveyard. She said it had been the loveliest day ever. She fell asleep then and he lay awake, listening to the engine throb, praying for Easter Sunday.

# ENGLISH PASTORAL

I met Patrick thirty years ago at college in Dublin. He was half-English. His life was a mess. We got on together, and when he left we kept in touch. Once on my way from London to Holyhead I stopped off to visit. He lived with his father, an old, thin man, who told me in a cold Irish voice that it was bad manners to call uninvited. The three of us sat together, silent, watching a black-and-white TV – it was the day Neil Armstrong landed on the moon. I still associate that with unhappiness. We wrote letters now and then, but the spaces between them grew longer. When he mentioned a woman recently – 'I'm staying with Joan …' – I was amazed but didn't ask. We've drifted apart. Who was she? How had it happened? What was their life together like?

What do people say behind our back? It's there, obvious, like our back, but we can't see it. We have to imagine.

September came in, the nights grew longer. By the second week the firework season had begun: first the small flat explosions like a carpet being beaten, then the heavier stuff. Gossamer covered Victoria Park in the morning, dead leaves covered the parked cars. Cars had their headlights on when they collected boys at Glen Prep School. The old ladies in Knapton Retirement Home left the garden benches to sit in the conservatory. Outside the railway station the Sikh taxi drivers' breath was white. Pallets were gathered for Guy Fawkes night. When the pubs closed, even the fights seemed part of the festival.

'Get him, Rodney!' A girl stood behind her boy, and Rodney sprang forwards – skinny jeans and pointy boots. The crack of his fist connecting was like a cue on a billiard ball. Orange street lights tinted his poppy, and blood spilling from the other boy's mouth.

Patrick said, 'It's like theatre.'

Joan's laugh was open – he saw the gums of her upper teeth. Someone asked her back for a nightcap but she said she had an early start next day. When the others had gone, she and Patrick walked to her car. It felt natural.

Imagine a man in his fifties, a virgin who wears a suit and tie although he has no job; who lives alone in the house where he was born, who went along one autumn night to the Local History Society meeting and met a woman – and it felt natural.

He had asked a question that showed more knowledge of local history than even Mrs Crier-Perry had. Joan had given him her gummy smile; afterwards he had bought her a drink. Under the table their knees had touched somehow. He had a voice and manner of confidence as heavy as his suit. She had a flat accent that put him at ease. They went on talking in the car as easily as they had in the Duke of Wellington. When she stopped outside his house he suddenly kissed her cheek, saying, 'Thank you, goodnight!' Her laugh went like a needle through his overcoat, jacket, jersey, shirt and thermal vest into his screwed-up heart. Then, just as he was getting out, she leaned over and kissed his mouth. A rocket hissed from a back garden and screamed up into an explosion of green sparks. He heard himself ask for her number, he saw her give him a card. He stood at his gate as she made a U-turn. She looked back as she drove away.

His brother called in as usual next morning. He had a dab of white ointment on a cold sore at the corner of his mouth. No greeting, as usual. He went into the kitchen, made tea and turned on the Radio 4 news. 'That bloody car is still there.' He stared out the window as he gulped his tea.

'It's Cresswell's.'

'Why doesn't he shift it? It's blocking our gate.' His brother rinsed his cup and walked out. Slam. These days he drove a Saab.

There were people like them in every town. They managed. They were just a bit out. It was a lack of energy, a confusion that came from the unhappiness in which they had been reared. A china duck sat on the mantelpiece with a barcode sticker still on its back. The woman who came in to clean didn't peel it off. They were odd.

His brother was an estate agent; his office was in the town. He worked hard all week, and at the weekend rode a horse. He had bursts of fearless aggression, and a wife who kept him calm. They looked after Patrick. One summer they had paid for him to go abroad on holiday, to see all those places he read about; but when Patrick arrived in Athens he had stayed in his hotel room for the week. His brother blamed it all on their mother – 'that fucking bitch' – who had walked out when they were young, on their father, who had sunk into depression, on the boarding school they had been sent to. They blamed all those things, but they were attached to them too.

Their father had been a doctor. That seems a simple fact. But imagine those days when a country shopkeeper scraped together the money to send his son to university. Imagine his parents' pride when he qualified, the state visit to the old family farm. His grandmother killed a chicken and gave it to him for luck. Imagine leaving De Valera's Ireland in search of work. Imagine joining the English middle class. He couldn't. He married his secretary, but she soon tired of his moods – he wanted her at home as his mother had been, he wanted her a lady about town – and she had left. But she had been glamorous, he had been a success, the sons had been to a famous Catholic school. With too much to lose by shaking off their past, they had ended up like this: half spider, half fly; half clinging to the sticky silk, half trying to escape. There are no simple people.

He went for his morning walk out the suburban roads, against the flow of people coming in to work. Always against the flow. Perverse. He wasn't stupid, he knew he was stuck in the past. He had said a firm *No*, though to him it was a *Yes*. *Yes* to the allowance from his brother, *Yes* to idleness, *Yes* to all the links of the chain that led back to their fucked-up home.

He was determined to hold onto it, to go on fucking it up. He had said a firm *No* to any other life, weak reproductions of the original mess. He had said *Yes* to *No*, *No* to *Yes*.

His brother had bought him a phone, in case of an emergency. One weekend, soon after the Athens disaster, he had gone to a country hotel outside the town. When his brother had found him missing he thought, not for the first time, *suicide*. When Patrick returned on Monday morning his brother released his anxiety. The years of shared unhappiness had made them close.

'Why didn't you tell me?'

'What?' He was blasé. He had managed, spent a weekend away from home.

'You obviously don't give a fuck!' Slam.

He sat in the park in his overcoat, watching a gardener at work, feeling the phone grow warm in his hand. How had it happened? Age? Exhaustion? Chance? – the car just running out of petrol and stopping at the Duke of Wellington. At lunchtime a shy Pakistani boy and girl in the grammar school uniform sat whispering on the opposite bench. When they had gone he rang her number; he was nervous, his voice filled with confidence. He said, 'You didn't think I'd call.' She laughed and said, 'You had to, hadn't you.' The confidence slipped from his shoulders, he felt a chill as if his overcoat had been pulled off.

He arrived too early at the restaurant, a new Italian one. It was empty. He felt a whisper of the old panic as he sat looking at a painting of big red tomatoes on the wall. Why was it so bad? Had any of the old masters painted tomatoes? Arcimboldo? Thinking made him calm. When she arrived, he stood and helped her take off her coat – formality might keep her away. But when she embraced him openly his body sank into her warmth. She was older and plainer than he had thought.

He knew his wine: he ordered Lacryma Christi, and explained what that meant. He explained what a fresco was. He was the fuddy-duddy eccentric scholar, his favourite role. But years of loneliness, panic, sadness, had given him awareness, and he listened as she talked of her job in the council office. When she mentioned the town she came from, he said his father had once done a locum there. She described her father's rough temper, how he used to knock her head against her brother's. He told her about his parents' divorce, his father's depression, the chain-smoking of cigarettes. She was interested and wanted to know more. It wearied him rather than upset him; he just said 'That was all long ago.' It was something that had hardened into a shape as fixed as the wine bottle. He filled her glass.

Her life saddened and fascinated him. As a girl she and her friends had made love with boys in the playing fields at night. She had never married, but she had lived with several men. But she hadn't gone out with anyone for years. She'd bought a cottage in the country; the mortgage would be paid by the time she retired.

She linked his arm as they walked to the high-rise car park. They kissed in the car. That, the excitement, talk and close company brought the old panic back. As she drove down the winding ramp to Cooke Street, he rolled down the window – 'Let in some air,' he said. She laughed. He talked openly of his neuroses – already he was backing out. His brother had once paid for him to see a psychiatrist, who said his panics came from 'fear of being smothered by mother love'. He couldn't remember even being touched by her. The drive home was a blur. But when he woke in the morning he felt the ease of her presence, and rang her at work. She was exhausted in the evenings but could meet him next weekend. He went for his usual walk.

He had spent so long not moving, that now he couldn't move. But he was also like a machine that goes on working, pistons pumping, cogs engaging, keeping everything as it is. Everything that happened could be fed into that machine. He was ruthlessly ineffectual.

Childhood visits with his father to Ireland, being away at school and university, then at a few dud jobs before trailing home had set him at a distance from his town. It was close but remote, like the country hills in the damp autumn sunlight out beyond London Road. He walked down to Queen Street and bought *The Daily Telegraph*. He walked up Orton Road and read it in the park. In the evening he had dinner in the chip café and chatted with the Turkish boy who worked there. He noticed the boy's new haircut – the sides were shaved, with patterns clipped into them – and he said they were like Neolithic rock carvings. The boy laughed. They all knew him. He was the old guy in the suit. He was OK. Bought flowers for the Oxfam shop girl on her birthday – phew! Didn't do ordinary. Nicer than his brother. That wouldn't be hard.

When he rang on Friday, she collected him outside the railway station after work. Her chin was red – she said his stubble had cut her skin when they had kissed. The girls in the office had guessed. She didn't care! A prostitute stood on the dark road behind the station as they drove out of town. Lonely men had to do with that. A woman was driving him to her house. But he was calm, confident he could fuck it up – the Oxfam girl hadn't spoken to him since the bunch of flowers. A Catherine wheel scattered blue sparks over the council estate. Then they were out of town. A leggy fox crossed their headlights and slipped into a trim hedge. Oak boughs black and heavy hung over the road. A small cricket ground and a small white pavilion lit up as she turned a bend.

He had a misfit's love of England, an imagined orderly place. If Ireland hadn't been stuck in the back of his mind, he mightn't have loved this place as much. The village was a narrow street of cottages huddled close together. A Royal Mail red sign jutted from an ivied wall, and a bigger sign showed there was a pub. It was called The Sack of Barley, the landlord knew her name, a single log three feet long blazed on the hearth. They had a glass of the local bitter with an old farmer and a big young man, his simple son. Then they walked up the dark street to her house.

She wasn't beautiful, she wasn't young, she was working class. And the chocolate velour sofa, the cosy-glow fire, the cheap gift shop pictures kept him at ease. She checked her phone messages; there was only one, a chirpy old woman's voice.

'My mother.' She took off her coat.

He sat in the middle of the sofa, spreading his arms along the back, so she had to sit in the armchair. They drank big gin and tonics, and she smoked cigarettes as they talked. She had lived in the north with an older man, but they'd had nothing in common apart from sex. She'd left him for another man down south, and though the sex hadn't worked she had loved him and stayed five years. But he had grown depressed, so she had left. She had once slept with a woman; it had felt strange, like touching yourself.

He had nothing like that to tell. He had fallen in love once when he worked in London. Or maybe it had just been an obsession. When they slept together he had been impotent.

'When was all that?'

'Twenty years ago.' He smiled, as if laying down a trump card.

'Jesus! That's scary!' she said.

They drank more gin and tonic and talked about the town, and the town where her mother lived, where his father had once worked. She looked at the clock when a church bell clanged. She had to be up early, she was too tired to drive him home, he could stay the night, but only as a friend. They went upstairs.

The ceiling sloped down to a low window. A high double bed took up most of the floor. When he went to the bathroom she called 'Shave!' His hand shook as he used the woman's razor. He refused when she offered to undress him. She turned off the light and lay quietly in bed. He opened the window to let in some air. Lying beside her he waited for her to move, and when she said, 'Let's just cuddle,' his body relaxed. She answered his kiss, and then his touch. When he grew in confidence, she drew gently away and lay still; then he drew close. When at last he succeeded he couldn't believe it. His sigh and hers chimed with the church bell striking one. He couldn't believe it.

He woke in the morning early when she got up for work. From the high soft bed he watched her dress and brush her hair. He had never seen anything like it. It was like a film. She told him to just pull the door shut when he was leaving; there was a bus stop at the end of the road. She kissed him and said she'd be in touch.

It was a film, and he was in it. He went to the post-office shop next door. The old woman behind the counter looked Indian. He bought the only *Telegraph*. An obituary of an eccentric clergyman went down well with tea, toast and marmalade, then he pulled the front door shut and walked down the street. A good Norman church, not restored. A manor house, sixteenth century, in a wooded park. The street ran out into a narrow road between fields of wheat stubble. Field mice, a partridge scuttled down the golden avenues. The film was called *Incredible*.

A fifteen-minute walk and he came to the main road. A ten-minute wait and the bus arrived.

The fields, the council estate, the suburb blurred into the town. He got out at Market Square. As if a glass had been wiped, everything seemed clear, the hills beyond London Road were close. When a girl walked before him, he noticed the gold creases behind her knees. He saw a letter teetering on the lip of a pillar box, tipped it in, and heard it drop. In five minutes he was home.

His brother came out of the kitchen. 'Where were you?' His thin face showed relief, then turned angry red. His upper lip looked raw, as if he'd shaved off a moustache. His wife came down the stairs. 'We didn't know where you were.'

'I met someone.'

'Who?'

He blushed as red as his brother. 'A friend.'

'Are you all right?' His brother looked at him closely.

'A bit tired. I might go to bed for an hour.'

His brother went out. Slam. His wife smiled and said, 'Give us a ring if you're staying out. You know how he is.' He noticed how good-looking she was.

When they had gone he rang the number. He could hear busy office noise. 'How are you?' he said.

She murmured 'My body is purring like a pussy cat.'

*Incredible.*

The week passed as usual. He went to the Thursday outdoor market, chatted with the Jamaican woman at the junk stall and bought a small scissors. Mrs Crier-Perry, who had always ignored him, gave him a sudden glance of her aquamarine eyes. He saw his reflection in the clothes stall mirror: he looked different. When he went for his nightly walk up Orton Road, a fox coming out of the park looked at him. He smiled and said, 'Good night.' The film couldn't get more incredible. It did. His brother called in to say he was going to the hotel outside town for the weekend; their dog was terrified by the fucking fireworks. Slam. When the Saab had gone he rang and invited her to dinner.

He walked down to Marks & Spencer's, bought a chicken, potatoes and a bottle of Pouilly-Fumé. Filled with warm cooking smells, the house felt strange. She rang to say she was at the gym and was running late. It was like being married. He ran upstairs and made his single bed. Her car headlights swept across the dining-room bay window. Her hair was wet from a shower, her face was pink. She looked at the plate he set before her and said 'Roast tatties, lovely!'

They ate and drank and talked, then suddenly it was too much. He wanted to lie down on the – what was it called? – like his brother's dog and sleep.

The kilim. He went on about the fireworks going through Harvest Thanksgiving, Guy Fawkes Night and Remembrance Sunday, but his face faded like the fire. It seemed to spark when she asked if he'd like to go to bed, but in bed he turned on his side to sleep. His guilt cleared when he heard her snore. The curtains flapped in the open window.

Next day was only Saturday. The weekend stretched before him like the empty London Road. As they walked round Victoria Park she said her mother wasn't well, she'd have to visit her that afternoon. His heart sprang up with relief. But it was only lunchtime. They had cold chicken sandwiches and the last of the wine. She was going, but every minute seemed an hour. He felt the breath of panic, as bad as when he had been in the Athens hotel room. Now, instead of lying in bed and clutching his pillow, he clutched her. They made love on the sitting-room floor. His knees were cut raw by the kilim.

'That was pretty heavy snogging,' she said. 'Good to let your feelings out.'

He said, 'I'll get your coat.'

'You don't like women to get too close.' She smiled. 'We must talk about it someday.'

He snapped, 'Why don't you talk about it to your *friends*!'

'Are you angry with me?'

He said, 'I'm sorry. It's my fault.' He was slipping, he didn't know what he was saying. As if he had a finger in one ear, he heard himself say, 'If you want to, you can slap my face.'

She looked at him for a moment, then she slapped his face. With the bleak smile his father used to give the gardener, he said, 'Would you like to do it again?'

She slapped him again, so hard that his head rang. She said, 'I feel more confident since I met you.'

'I'm glad.'

'You're a strange one, you are.' She embraced him. 'We might try a little more of that next weekend.' She waved as she drove away.

The silence he had longed for rang in his head like the pain of her slaps. He cleared the table and washed up. He had been stupid, he had forgotten what he was. A mess. He could no more change that than change the colour of his eyes. He cried when he saw the empty bed, then smoothed the sheet and pillow, and drew up the cover. He put the chicken carcass in the Marks & Spencer's bag, brought it up to the park and left it in the bushes for the fox. She rang in the evening, but he didn't reply. She rang again on Friday, and again he let it ring out. When she didn't ring again he was disappointed but relieved.

He returned to his old routine. He had done it before, he could do it again. His brother took him to dinner in the hotel outside town. His sister-in-law smiled and asked about his friend. His brother told him to be careful, they only wanted to protect him. It only made him worse.

He didn't shave some mornings, didn't even dress. Sometimes he stayed inside all day in his blue-and-white-striped pyjamas. When she called to the house one evening, he said he wasn't well and went back upstairs. She followed. She looked at a crucifix on the wall above his bed, laughed and spread out her arms. He looked at her coldly, and she left. It was winter when he went out again, his overcoat open, his scarf flapping, like a split beast trailing its insides.

His legs took him to her office; she came downstairs and stood at the door. She seemed old, there were dark rings under her eyes. She told him to come back when he knew what he wanted. Half spider, half fly, how could he know that? He couldn't go forwards, he couldn't go back. But the old spider was afraid. He had done something it had never expected, found a way to break the web. He didn't see that he had been breaking it for years, in everything he did: losing touch with Ireland, wandering about the town, chatting with the gardener in the park, the Turkish boy in the chip café, the Jamaican woman at the junk stall. There were only a few strands left.

One Thursday at the outdoor market in the square he heard the news of her mother's death.

There weren't many at the funeral. She looked up when he arrived. Her brother wore a black leather cap through the service, and said, 'I have to scoot after the crem.' Alone together later they cleared out her mother's house. He told the Jamaican woman, who took away things for her stall. When he brought sacks of clothes to the Oxfam shop, the girl gave him a scowl. One evening when they had finished, they drove to the village outside the town.

It was a spring evening, the kind that makes you open windows again, when you notice suddenly the soft light and expectant air, the buds beginning to blur the bare outlines of the trees. As they walked down the narrow street, there was a smell of wood smoke and cold, fresh clay. They stood to watch a blackbird on a garden wall shriek at a stalking cat. The church door was open, the light shone in across a sunken flagstone floor. He felt a return of the old panic, as if he'd missed a step of a stairs in the dark. He felt everything was slipping away.

They went into The Sack of Barley, and there was the wood fire that made the smoke. They had a glass of the local bitter with the old farmer and the big young man, his simple son, who talked about dogs and shooting. The landlord said he had a couple of partridge in the deep freeze, they could have them for dinner if they liked; he was developing the cuisine side of his trade. They said they'd be back that night.

A silver wisp, a new moon, had risen in the pale sky. Walking back to her cottage they talked about the farmer's simple son. She said it was sad the way he looked at her, a pity he had no girlfriend of his own. He agreed. He said he was sorry he was a washout, that he couldn't give her any more. When she cried he caressed the nape of her neck with his hand.

The post-office shop was still open, and there was the *Telegraph*. He sat on the chocolate velour sofa, reading while she lay in the bath. He wasn't able for it, it was too much. But first they could have dinner in the pub. His belly sank against his belt, he pictured her breasts slipping to either side. That's how the skin grows old, the spirit grows strong and supple, that's how a human being is made. He heard the bathwater run out, the slap of her bare feet on the floor. He counted the church bell's quick clangs. There are no simple people. There are no simple people.

# WEEKENDS IN DEPTFORD

Friday evening in Deptford. Council workers sweeping the High Street, melting ice in the gutters smelling of fish; Africans and West Indians calling to each other as they locked up; strange bird screams and whistles from the shuttered pet shop. Two Scotsmen were drinking and shouting on the plinth around the old anchor. A big Irish Traveller boy tried to sell me a Rolex watch. Weekend traffic pounded down Creek Road. Children played in the garden between the blocks of flats. No greeting, not even a glance, from someone coming down the concrete stairs. A glimpse from the top balcony of the trees on Greenwich Hill.

Her door was left open, she was sitting at the table smoking a cigarette, just saying 'Ah ...' when I came in. It was small, with a few nice things from the flea market, and an old kilim brought back from somewhere on the floor – nothing she couldn't leave. Trains for Charing Cross rattled past the window. The double-glazing panel leaned against the wall. I said, 'You promised to put it back.'

'I won't jump. I just like to know I can.' She topped the cigarette, smiled and stood up. 'I prepared supper.'

I used to think she might have been happy if she had married, had a husband, a home; that her life had been an assertion of self, an effort beyond her power, that had worn her out. But that was my thinking. How do you know?

We argued about the right way to make salad dressing, and drank the Sainsbury's wine I brought. Elbows on the table, her chin on the heels of her hands, she talked about her cancer treatment, and gave out about her son – he was so stupid, he had been in prison for smuggling drugs. She looked ready to talk all night. By nine o'clock I'd had enough, and said I'd take a walk. She gave me the door key and shuffled into her bedroom. She was easy to stay with. You came and went as you pleased.

We had met in the eighties, teaching English abroad, and since then I visited her every year.

I liked those evening walks, seeing the changes in that place I had come to know. The library swimming pool complex had opened. The ruined side street was still waiting to be knocked down. There was a new Cash For Gold shop. After all her travelling and adventures she had settled in the sort of place she came from.

She came from a poor part of Birmingham. Her father worked in a factory, and at sixteen she had a job as a typist there. At eighteen she had a boyfriend who wanted to marry her, but she was different. One morning on the bus to the factory she couldn't face the life she saw ahead. She bought a suitcase, and told her parents she had to leave. I imagined them, used to acceptance, standing at the door to watch her walk down the street. She took the train to Dover; by evening she was in Paris, alone and free. That had been fine when she was young and everything was new. Now she was old, looking at that open window. She had paced the distance to it like a footballer measuring the run-up to a kick.

There was an ordered side to her: you didn't lie on in bed. At seven in the morning the smells of cigarette smoke and coffee seeped into my room. While I had breakfast she sat in silence – if you had nothing to say you didn't speak. That suited me. One Saturday her son called in, a quiet, middle-aged, dark-skinned man. She spoke to him the way she did to me, as acquaintances do when they meet.

'Are you back with that band?'

'Yea.'

'How's Joy? Is she still in the salon?'

'She is. Yea.'

'I haven't seen the girls for a while. Why don't you send them over some day?'

'Yea. I will.' He fetched a music tape from his old room, the room where I stayed. He said, 'See yo, Mum' as he left. His voice was a mix of BBC and Black street-talk.

Saturday had been her lover's day, when I'd had to go out for the afternoon. I never met him but knew he was Black: she could sleep only with Black men, she said. He gave her money before they went to bed – it was part of his fantasy that she was a white whore. Afterwards they discussed philosophy and drank the champagne she had bought. And when he killed himself she told me how: he swallowed sleeping pills and put his head in a plastic bag. I guessed that was the end of sex. She went for walks with me instead.

We used to walk south-east London through places I had never been, going down the Greenwich Tunnel and coming up in the Isle of Dogs. We talked as we sat in sordid pubs. She liked Channel 4 News, but only with Jon Snow. She disliked my writing – 'It's flat.' Her sister in Birmingham had been in touch. When I said, 'I'll wander off for a bit,' she accepted that. She was tolerant in the English way, which seemed detached. Once, buying *The Guardian*, she bought a top-shelf magazine for me. It was like a statement: you do what you choose. She once said, 'We'll be friends for as long as it goes, and if it runs out, well that's it.'

She was eighteen when she ran away to Paris. She stayed in a cheap hotel, where at breakfast, a bowl of milky coffee and a cut of baguette, she made friends with another English resident. One night she was so lonely that she knocked on his door: he was an artist, who explained what calling to a man's room at night usually meant. She went back to her room. But through him she found work as an artist's model, which she grew to hate: she said it took away your soul, the only time I heard her use that word. She met other models and sat with them in cafés, listening to their talk. One day, after a year or so, all the words came together and made sense. When she opened her mouth she spoke in French.

She knew artists, she spoke French – it went on. She met an old bourgeois Frenchman who took her in. The other girls laughed among themselves but in fact she never slept with him: she said she was frigid, and he understood. I felt it was a time of confusion, when she was both protected and growing up. When he died she learnt with wonder that he had left his apartment to her.

She had left home to escape the working class, the boss, industrial ugliness, sadness – now at last she could spread her wings abroad. When she fell in love with a young Black man, it felt she was entering another world. That ended soon: she became pregnant, and he went back to his wife. The old Frenchman had children, who contested his will and won. They gave her money, that didn't last long. Then she was homeless in Paris with a son.

We saw him pass by one day in Deptford – a curly grey beard, Rasta plaits – and she said when his father had told her he was married, a thud went down her stomach.

She wouldn't go home: young spirit, pride, the memory of Birmingham didn't allow a return. With her English and her typing she found a job in UNESCO, where she did well. When they offered promotion, which meant going to Africa, she agreed. As they paid for her son's education, she sent him back to England to a liberal public school. She had failed, but he would succeed. She worked in Ethiopia, Kenya, Congo – every few years she was transferred. Her difference marked her out. Her last post was in

Freetown, the poorest place on earth. There, as if something had hardened in her, she resigned.

Her taste for the ordinary had gone, like muscles left unused. Her son hardly knew her, and she hardly knew him. He begged her to take him from the good school, where he couldn't fit in; but when they got a flat in Deptford he ran wild and left. As an English teacher she went abroad again. That was when we met.

She used to sit alone in the staffroom at tea break, smoking cigarettes, sighing out the smoke, then shuffling in her sandals and long, shapeless skirt back to class. Her shabbiness and depression irritated the local teachers. They said, 'Why doesn't she make an effort? She's not so old.' Once when they played a folk music tape, she tried to join in, swaying her arms above her head as they did. She seemed so wooden, ridiculous, I had to look away.

But we had English in common and used to talk in the bus after school. By then she had taught in Algeria, Iran, Morocco; in each she had been 'more or less raped'. She had slept with so many men she hadn't liked, she said, that it didn't make much difference to have to sleep with a few more. To me it suggested something missing or dead. She had grown up with a low sense of herself? Been crushed by the life she had had? Those were other things

I couldn't say. You can't sum up someone's life in a few words.

That didn't end our closeness; in fact she entered my life a little more. As I had visited her, I wanted to invite her in return. My uncle had died and left me his house in Mayo, where I used to stay some weekends. When I suggested she come to visit, she agreed. I went to meet her at Knock Airport.

I remember the local pride when it was built, the lads speeding cars down the runway, celebrating their connection to the big world. Curlews cried and flew away as the Ryanair plane came in to land. Wind blew the smell of jet fuel through the furze flower scent. Emigrants home on holiday came down the stairs. Seeing her shuffle across the tarmac, I realised that she was my first visitor: because I liked to be alone there, but also because I was ashamed of my uncle's poor little farm. It was to me what Birmingham was to her. There is always a reason for friendship.

In the morning she made her special coffee in a small dirty saucepan she had brought. Then she went out to explore, as she had when she lived abroad, making another start in another place. She returned a few hours later, bright with news: 'I met a nice man called Mike …' I knew him, an old bachelor like my uncle, alone in a ruined house. His littered garden, the cow tethered by a bit of clothes line were nothing new to her. 'It's like Greece, messed up,' she said.

When we went out next day he was waiting, lonely, eager to talk. She talked to him the way she talked to her son, the dealers in Deptford flea market, me, anyone. He talked about England, where he had worked, and his regret that he had ever come back. He said, 'The English are awful straight. You know where you stand with them. In England there was no worse man to work for than the Irishman.'

She said, 'Life's a mess if you live it, and if you don't it's a bore.'

'Well now you said it.'

I took her down the boreen, under the stunted alder trees, between the bracken and foxgloves that grew from deep banks of moss. Springs seeping from the wet fields made a stream that rattled down a stony bed into a small lake. I loved to swim in its soft water stained gold by the turf banks along the shore: for me that was pure home, a place where I remembered who I was. For her it was just another place that she would leave. Silent, detached, she sat smoking cigarettes. It got me down. One day I said, 'You're too absorbed in yourself.'

'I've had that sort of facile remark before,' she snapped, and I drew back. We had never argued. I was relieved when she left.

In London, gradually, she became more herself. People born a little different – in character, class, colour, who knows what – often continue down that road to a stubborn individualism. Each time I visited I saw it grow. She began to pick cigarette ends from the street to smoke – 'Why not?' she said when she saw my look. To make money now, she worked for drug companies that gave her a few hundred pounds to take what they had tried on rats or mice. What did she swallow in those weekends at the laboratory hostel? She didn't know, or care. When she tried to kill herself, it was in the same indifferent way: she swallowed a bottle of Boots aspirin. They didn't work. That was when she took the double-glazing panel from her window.

Her parents had never gone to church, and nor had she. I sometimes went to Deptford chapel, built long ago by Irish immigrants, where the congregation now was mostly Black. When I mentioned that one Sunday, she asked to come along. The Mass meant nothing to her, I could see – it was like some foreign film without subtitles. But the women's brilliant gowns and headdresses, their children's hair in shining cornrow plaits, their swaying and rhythm as they sang made her smile like a girl. As we left the chapel she said, 'Oh I liked that!'

'It's on every week, if you want to go.'

She shrugged, and eyed the pavement for cigarette ends.

It was one of those Sunday evenings when we were sitting in the flat. We had our argument about salad dressing, and finished the Sainsbury wine I brought. Around nine o'clock I said I'd take a walk, but she said, 'Please don't go.' She had never said such a thing before. She didn't want to be alone; I wanted to get out. We compromised – she came with me.

She was old now, and still had cancer, but she shuffled along as ever, determined, keeping up. We went through Deptford and down New Cross Road. I couldn't imagine her living in Chelsea or Knightsbridge: they were as remote to her as Freetown was to me. She was at home among the grimy stucco houses broken into flats, the exotic-dancer pub, the car wash, the carpet showroom with the big smashed window. Swooning Arab music blew from passing cars. At Sainsbury's she took my arm and said we'd cross the road.

In ten minutes we were walking up a steep hill into a different world. The roots of tall plane trees rippled the pavement, so she had to walk carefully. The front gardens were gently wild, the doors were painted in refined, smoky shades. Warm night air brought out the sweet scent of jasmine. Someone was playing a cello. Even the rubbish was good. She saw a rug left out for collection, unrolled it and found no stains. She said, 'We'll take it on the way back.'

'Where are we going?'

'I want to show you where my son lives.'

At the top of the steep road we came to Telegraph Hill. From there you could see London light up slowly, as though a tide was coming in. Blackbirds were still singing, feral parakeets were screeching as they flew from tree to tree. A scent of sun-dried grass breathed from the park. She stopped outside iron railings and pointed to an elegant modern house with big windows and varnished timber walls screened by tall bamboo. She whispered, 'It's social housing, but very good.'

'How did he get that?'

'He has Joy behind him.'

I had heard of her, his partner, who had a hair salon. A strong Black Christian, she had taken him in hand. Two girls appeared at a lighted window – 'My grandchildren' – she whispered again, as if they might hear. As she looked at them I saw longing in her eyes, but she caught my arm and drew me away. Joy disapproved of her, thought she was bad for him; that was why he and the children no longer called. It would cause trouble if she was seen snooping around.

It was more than that. Her home was in the dark, outside. Being a scavenger suited her in the same way. As we went back down the hill, she stopped to take the rug. She said, 'It's just the right size for my front room.'

'But you have one.'

'This one is different.'

It was heavy, and I grew irritable as we carried it down to New Cross Road. All those thoughts I had never said came up. I wanted to say that she hadn't found another world anywhere because she had never changed; that she had slept only with Black men because she felt like them, poor outsiders; that her son was right to stay away from her dreams of escape. But how could I say any of that? Drawing back, I just said, 'Why do you have to be different?' Even that was too much.

'What does that mean?' She snapped again.

It was an argument about everything, without any words. It went on in silence as we sat together in the bus back to Deptford. Her face was still cold when we reached the flat. She took up the kilim and spread the new rug on the floor. It was big and loudly exotic, but it fitted perfectly. As if to make her point, she said, 'You see?'

'I prefer the other one.'

'Would you like it?'

'I would.' And I did. It was beautiful, simple – dark shapes set inside a border of faded blue and grey pink. She smiled as she rolled it up for me.

The row was over, we talked peacefully until late. Then she went into her bedroom and changed, went to wash in the bathroom and returned. Her white cotton nightdress came down to her feet. Barefoot, she was small. Combed out, her long grey hair touched the small of her back. She stopped at the door. 'You know I have cancer?'

'I know.'

'I've had a breast removed.'

I said 'You never told me that.'

She drew down her nightdress shyly to show me the hollow scar. I glimpsed her other breast, soft and whole. She had left her past to make another life? You could say that about anyone, I could say it about myself. But she had done it completely – cut herself off. As she went into her room and shut the door, I could see her setting out alone sixty years ago. Next morning I went home with the old kilim under my arm. I never saw her again.

She didn't have to jump out the window: cancer carried her away the following year. I rang the hospital when she was dying. Her son was there. She couldn't speak but was conscious, he said. He said my name and put the phone in her hand. I spoke to a silence – not even the sound of her breathing – then he took the phone and said goodbye in his quiet Black, street-talk BBC voice.

# AN EVENING PROWL

What had been small things once turned out to be big things later on. It hadn't been important that her family was Protestant, that their land was good, that she had gone to a different school and played different games. All that had been as natural as the farm.

Nothing seemed to change here: a blackbird was washing in a puddle outside the grain shed, withered leaves drifted from the hawthorn hedge; but things changed here, as everywhere. Cries came from the cow house, the blackbird shook drops of water from his back and flew screeching over the hedge, and that night he was roosting somewhere else.

## An Evening Prowl

A young bullock not properly castrated had put a two-year-old heifer in calf. They used the jack to help her labour, and when all came well they went up to the house for breakfast. She was eating the afterbirth when they looked in again, and Susan's father said it was the calf's turn now. He lifted the small wet heifer sprawled on the straw, straightened her rubbery forelegs, held her between his knees and put her nose to the mother's teats. She wouldn't suck. He took a teat and squirted milk on her nose, but the calf drew away. He squeezed again, and the calf sucked, then let the teat slip from her mouth. When he squeezed a third time, the calf fastened on the teat and sucked with noise. Tommy said, 'Isn't nature a great thing.' He was the workman. He called a teat a spin.

He swept the cobbled channel out to a tidy heap of straw manure. Susan washed their nylon pull-ups and hung them on a line in the hay shed. Her father scrubbed the jack and stood it in the sun. They left their boots outside the back door, washed and dressed, then drove to church, where they sat in the front bench. There was a small stained-glass window with her mother's family coat of arms, but she disliked the rector and did not attend. When they came home, she had dinner prepared. Tommy was back from Mass, eating in the kitchen – that had been natural too, and her father calling to him through the dining room's open door.

'Will you bring in those yeowes this evening?'

'It'd be no harm.'

A low winter sun lit up the room for ten minutes: the alloy beakers of home-made lemonade, the battered silver on the sideboard, the Victorian photo portraits and the spear from Africa on the wall. As the sun slid behind the trees, Susan said, 'I'd better go.'

Her mother embraced her firmly, her father took her suitcase out to the car. Tommy called 'God bless!' and rapped his knuckles on the bonnet. She was used to this Sunday departure, the drive along back roads, the glimpses through bungalow windows of families gathered about a bright TV. It had been natural that she hadn't known them well. Outside the railway station there were the usual half-dozen cars. A lost curlew's cry came through the misty dark. In two hours she was at Dublin Airport, and over London in two hours more. Miles of red tail lights wound like giant intestines along the motorways. She was back in her routine.

Her father accepted that she might never live with them again. He hoped that his son would come home one day. He himself had come from England and married into a family long settled here: Susan had his slow manner, with a mute form of her mother's assurance. At church they met old neighbours, and through a shared sense of a small difference they met newcomers – English, German, Dutch. Tommy was the only local she really knew. Once when he was ploughing she had seen the tractor stop, the big tyres sink in the green spring turf: a newborn hare had been lying ahead. She had watched him take it up and place it in a furrow and go on ploughing. And now she was in London. She rang her parents every week.

They had been uneasy at her leaving, but thought it best that she learnt to live in the world. They had seen her at country parties, her face bright red after a single drink. She had no sense of clothes but had a physical air that attracted boys. A young soldier – British, home on leave – had asked her out, and she had gone though her father had said, 'Better not.' He had said it again when she wanted to go to the crossroads pub, but again she had gone, and overheard the murmur, 'What's she doing here?' She had persisted and met a local, who enjoyed her eager body, then withdrew in puritan confusion. She had been hurt by that – the small things were becoming bigger things. After church one Sunday morning a neighbour had mentioned friends who were looking for an au pair girl. They lived in Corfu, they kept horses – would Susan be interested? In the same way she had gone out with the soldier and gone to the pub, she had taken the job. And now she was married to Alex.

They owned a semi-detached house of ginger brick in a south London suburb. It was the best they could afford, and from her slow nature, from generations of prosperity, she had an almost hostile indifference to 'getting on'. When an aunt had left her money they could have put a deposit on a better house, but they stayed. She had the attic made into a bedroom for their daughter, and the garage into a studio for Alex. He was a graphic designer.

'And how's old Ireland?' His greeting was always the same, and his moving around the kitchen, making a sandwich while they talked. The radio was always on, usually 5 Live. Sometimes he talked back to it in his twangy London voice: 'Well, they're economic migrants, aren't they.' He had wires everywhere, connecting a VHF cable to the kitchen radio and to another radio in his studio. He wanted a good reception. He liked cycling. He followed Millwall. Her mother had wondered at their marriage, but tried to accept it as natural. Hadn't she herself married outside their small community, bringing in fresh blood to their dull, good land?

Because he didn't make enough money, Susan worked as an assistant in the local school. From her window she heard trains rattle behind the green wire fence, and saw the red morning sun blurred by the city's haze. She took it all for granted now, as she did the spray paint remarks – *Sluts 'R Us* – on the playground wall. From her father, and from visiting English cousins, she slotted in. She was used to the stiffening in the English, their not rushing to agree. She grew used to the London impersonal cordiality. It was a language she had learnt. Alex spoke it too.

She had liked her job in Corfu, minding children in a country house. There were the same hymns at church on Sunday, the warm smells of horses and manure – it had been like summer time at home. But the children's parents had treated her like a servant, and on her free day she escaped to a local town, wandering through the market under vines trained over a dusty street. She had stopped to buy a kebab; Alex had been standing at the same stall. He had come for a family wedding, he was staying with cousins for a week. She had told him about her job. They had stood there talking easily in the smell of burning fat and charcoal smoke. He had walked with her to the bus stop in the evening, they had kissed under a wild fig tree growing from a wall. It had been natural and strange. Apart from her slight Irish accent and his olive skin each seemed English through and through, but each had picked up the other's small difference. His parents were from

Corfu, and lived in London now. She had joined him there when she left her job.

In marrying her he had moved up a social step; in him she had met someone brighter. His mind was lively, full of facts from the radio and newspapers. Hers was simple, deliberate: she had to grasp each fact before she could go on. When he was sent some botched graphic work by an Irish firm, he said, 'What an abortion!' and laughed. She asked what was wrong with it, slowing him down, making him think. He pushed her on, gave her something to think about. Though his parents lived a few miles away, he didn't see any more of them than she did of hers. He had gone with her a few times to Ireland, but that soon stopped. London was the centre of his world – he had an incomer's need to belong. She didn't know that need. She had felt like a mould in which he fitted.

She hadn't any wish to be different: their house was like the others on the road, with a small front garden and plastic chairs on a back patio. Like other neighbours they had two children. The residents' association had put her in charge of the allotments. She had bought an apple tree in the supermarket, which at first she thought would never do, but now it was ten feet tall, overshadowing Alex's studio. He spent the day in there.

## An Evening Prowl

With his radios and newspapers, his mind seemed like their front garden full of scraps blown in off the road; but in the studio everything was ordered. Each box of paper was labelled and arranged on shelves. The glass worktop was as clean as the window; there were dust covers on the computer, scanner and printer. His collection of *Penthouse* and *Mayfair* magazines was in a neat stack on the floor. His telephone, Millwall mug and radio were on a low table by his armchair. Though he went out with a cycling club, the S.E. Wheelers, on Saturday mornings, he didn't have close friends. As she had turned the garage into a studio, he had turned it into a nest.

Lifting the phone one Sunday evening to ring home, she heard him on his extension talking to a woman, English, she could tell by the voice. Their intimate words confused her; she felt she was living with a stranger. She didn't mention it – how could she say she had been listening in? A woman called to the door one day, a customer, he said and brought her into the studio. She answered the door another day, and there was a girl with bright eyes and blush make-up. She brought her into the kitchen, made tea and called him on his extension. The women stopped calling then, but she regretted that because now she didn't know what was going on.

She had to guess what was going on when he moved fast around the kitchen in good form. He'd say business was going well, he read out bits on global warming from the paper. She heard his shrill laugh when he talked with customers on the phone. Sometimes he tuned in to Classic FM. In his red Nike tracksuit and trainers he looked more like a son than a husband, but he looked his age when whatever was going on ended, and he was depressed for days. She saw the strain in their children's faces when he slept in his studio armchair. She tried to understand, to reach him.

When her mother came to visit, she noticed how he and Susan moved around each other, never touching. She saw her shove one of his magazines under a cushion and murmur, 'I wish you wouldn't leave these in here.' She saw her lower lip jut out, her confused frown. When she asked if he could turn down the radio, he jumped up dramatically and switched it off. Her mother was somebody at home, but that assurance bounced off him. She said, 'You need a good kick in the pants.' He told her to get back on her broomstick and go home. When he flounced out, she said, 'Silly ass.' Susan explained that he was highly strung. They watched him shoot out the gate on his Jaws bike, in his black

## An Evening Prowl

Lycra tights, black helmet and cycling goggles. The children said he looked like a big bluebottle.

But it could be wonderful at bedtime after those scenes, if they had made up, when he watched her fold her blouse, skirt and tights, unclip her pearl earrings and put them in the little drawer, then rub cold cream into her hands. His black hair grew not just in the usual places but on his shoulders and back. His furious lovemaking could still bring her to life.

He grew more confident or wilder. He bought a car, an old Rover, they couldn't afford. He made friends with a neighbour, a Hungarian woman, who was soon dropping in to visit. She had a dead look in her eyes and a squat body that gave off a disturbed air. They were sharing a bottle of wine one night, he was buzzing around, full of chat, when the woman suggested they all sleep together. Susan's upbringing had taught her not to be afraid of herself: she could enjoy the touch of those cool Hungarian hands, even his nervous excitement. But as they moved about in the bed and the woman took charge, his breath became panting and the disturbed air felt evil. Susan said she wouldn't do that again.

He said you couldn't get spare parts for the Rover, and traded it in for an old Volvo 3L. He said Britain was going down the drain. He told her it was Salvador Dalí, not Salvador Daly. He said the Turks were barbarians. At dinner he'd tell her to wipe her mouth. There could be rows about anything. She said in her mute way that she didn't care if he was rich or poor, weak or strong; she'd live with him in a tent but she wanted a human relationship. If he couldn't give that, then she'd go somewhere else. It was a speech she had prepared. He told her to do what she liked, that he certainly did. She stopped sleeping with him after that. She had to.

Under a vague sense of herself she had a firm sense of right and wrong. It allowed her to answer a Lonely Hearts ad in the local free paper. The man was small and made her laugh. He brought her to a greyhound track, where they sat in the stand drinking lager and watching the electric hare whizz round. But her manner confused him; she was both open and distant. He simply held her hand. She felt nothing, and didn't meet him again.

The Hungarian woman no longer called in. Alex said he didn't see her now, but Susan felt that she had opened some door he couldn't shut. By the time she learnt he had a girlfriend, her first feeling was relief: it made him calmer, or contained his moods at least. When he went away at weekends she had her own life. On Saturday the allotments committee met. On Sunday morning she went to church, a nonconformist one she had found, where the minister – in a plain black suit, white shirt and black tie, with a head of fine silver hair – gave a sermon full of thought and feeling. If God was almighty, then why was there evil in this world? The only answer was that God was weak, as his son Jesus was weak; but that sacrifice to the power of the world was the way of eternal life. A man sitting beside her stifled sobs, his shoulders shook. He had the same straight nose as her father's. She cried too when they stood and sang the hymn.

Then it was evening and Alex was back, moving around the kitchen, talking about the news. One evening he mentioned his girlfriend's name, Ede. He began to mention her in conversation, as if he wanted her accepted. She was Nigerian. She was a travel agent. She'd been in London for twenty years. Soon she was part of their life, like his radios and newspapers, his Saturday morning cycle with the Wheelers, and still his moods.

He had fallen out with his parents but liked Susan to visit them, so she did. They had tea in a spotless small sitting room, where his mother showed framed photos of him as a boy: stiff in a school blazer and cap, lost in whites with a big cricket bat. His father talked about the good old days in Corfu, the Royal Navy where he had been a cook, and the restaurant he had opened in London, where Alex had refused to work. Because he was sensitive, his mother said. Their accents showed through when they argued. Susan felt that their hard-working immigrant life had been only part of his life, that part of his life had been beyond them; maybe beyond him too. Afterwards, seeing her to the door, his mother asked, 'How is he?' as if the truth could only be told when they were alone. It helped her to understand him.

Look at him out cycling with the Wheelers, pushing up Greenwich Hill. He stopped at the Observatory for five minutes and stood astride the Meridian Line, the centre of the world. Then, standing on the pedals, his olive forehead shining with sweat, he cut across Blackheath to catch up. He was dissatisfied unless he had seen or done something he hadn't seen or done before. The smallest thing would do: learning that this path was a shortcut to that road was proof his time had not been wasted, and he was going forwards not back. He had to keep going. He had to.

When she came home one evening he was working in a corner of the kitchen. 'It's a bit claustro in the studio,' he said. Each day she came home he seemed to have taken up more space, like a cuckoo in a nest. She grew used to his papers spreading on the table, his Millwall mug of tea. To argue wasn't in her nature; she was used to reserve, living slightly apart, caution. There were times when her father had the chance to buy more land, but didn't because it might have angered the locals. Her nature was to manage.

She felt that angered him – she saw it in his eyes. She was right. He hated her quiet voice and patience, the way she sat there like Lady Muck watching him fly around in circles, waiting for him to return. Well he wouldn't, no way, he needed his freedom. But that brought the thought, What would life be like without her waiting quietly there? The empty answer filled him with fear. He felt that something in him was buried; that below, out of reach, with no connection to above, there was a pool of life deeper even than the Hungarian woman had revealed. To reach it was more than he was able: he was often terrified of what he might find down there. *Terrified* was far from expressing his feeling; it was beyond words, like falling into endless space. Her presence kept him from that. He hated that. When he felt like that, he went to stay with Ede for the weekend.

Ede was different. She saw herself as his future wife, though he had made clear that this would never be. Meanwhile, he gave her money, and prestige: it was important to her that she was seen linking a white man's arm. In return she gave him sex. He disliked everything about her: the sword-blade eyebrows and lilac lipstick, the swooning airs. She said, 'You're going to lose me if you're not careful!' when he turned on the TV.

'Yeah, there's nothing on.' He felt on the carpet for the remote.

'This came in.'

'What's that?' He went to the kitchen and got a beer from the fridge. They were like any middle-aged couple. She wore her glasses openly. He looked out the window as she explained. There was a good offer on plane tickets to Nigeria; he could meet her mother and daughter there. To get him on the tarmac in Lagos – that was her dream. She smiled and stood before him, pressing her breasts to his chest.

'Nice.'

'My daughter says they are my greatest asset.'

'How is she?'

'She's fine. You'll see. How's Susan?' She turned and wagged her bottom.

'Same old.' He drank his beer. 'Better hit the road.'

'But you've only just come.'

'Things to do. I just looked in to say hi.'

Her eyes followed his hand as he felt in his pocket. A frown split her forehead when he took out his car keys. She said, 'You're some operator!' – her eyes flashed like her sequinned blouse. She'd scrape his face if it helped, but it wouldn't. He had the power. She tilted up her face for his kiss. He gave a low whistle of relief as he went down the stairs.

What did Ede give him that she couldn't give? What went on in his mind? Susan tried to answer those questions in bed at night. Not peace, anyway. She heard him in his bed across the landing, turning on his back, on his side. He heard her snore, then he fell asleep, angry still. She gave him the confidence to be unfaithful.

She went home to see her parents more often, and brought the children when their summer holidays came. A blackbird washed in the dust outside the grain shed; green leaves filled the hawthorn hedge. The small heifer calf had grown to a fine cow with calves of her own. She was sold, and one of the calves was served. Susan sat with her mother after breakfast, catching up with the news. The cranky German basket-maker had moved to South Africa, not far from the ranch where her brother worked. The Dutch organic farmer had run away with a local girl. Best of all, the rector had retired. She helped her father to count cattle and bring in the sheep to be sheared. On Sunday they went to church, where she met their old neighbours, people like themselves. They laughed loudly, were wise with money, had a firm view of life. It came from responsibility to their good land, that they had inherited, maintained and would pass on.

There was piped water from a group scheme that her mother had organised, but for drinking they preferred their own spring. Clay from a ditch bank and leaves had fallen into it, and stones from the lane. One evening they went to clean it out. Tommy was growing old but he stayed to help. She still loved the scent of his cigarette smoke in the open air, of meadowsweet on the other side of the ditch, the drone of a May bug passing in the dusk. But they were all part of the most beautiful feeling, people working together: handing each other the shovel, passing up buckets of muck to be thrown away, holding Tommy's shoulder as he reached in, sharing the weight of a boulder that had fallen from the well's walling and had to be set back in place. Then they put their hands down into the deep cold to feel the spring surge up freely.

Her children helped her mother to make tea, butter the currant bread and bring it out on a tray. Tommy put his hands on their shoulders and said, 'The men and women of tomorrow, when we'll be in the clay.' Beautifully tired, peaceful, they watched the moon rise in the east, where London was, picking out the snowberries in the hedge like a thousand little moons. They stood by the well until it was dark. No one wanted to leave. Tommy said, 'That'll be settled by morning. Ye can drink it then.'

Another evening he told them that his niece was playing music in the crossroads pub. Susan said she'd like to go along. Her father didn't speak, but her mother said a brisk 'Why not?' The Troubles were over now.

The pub looked deserted except for a tractor outside. She was excited when she went in: everything was as familiar and strange as London. An old man sat by an empty fireplace; a smell of Jeyes Fluid from the toilet blew across a new extension floor. A red-haired boy was playing pool on a lavish green table, a white-haired woman was serving behind the bar. Tommy sat up at the counter with his pint of beer.

Slowly the pub began to fill. Tommy's niece arrived with two friends, whom he introduced shyly to Susan. Her own face reddened when Seamus came in, the local she had once slept with. She was glad when the music began. The white-haired woman turned the TV down, and the world's news played out silently to the tune of a violin, a flute, a melodeon. The young women swayed to the music as if they wanted to dance, but their men stood straight together, intent on drink and talk. The old man by the fireplace said, 'When I was yeer age I'd dance on a tombstone' – and then Seamus asked Susan to dance.

He said he was married now, with children, but he still thought of her, she hadn't changed. She still enjoyed his quick intimacy and witty talk. As they danced and talked she felt at home with him, with Tommy and his niece and her friends, with the white-haired woman, and the red-haired boy sitting on the edge of the pool table swinging his legs, with this place she didn't really know. Rain was hammering on the flat roof of the extension. She felt as she had when they had cleaned the well, and the water had surged up freely. He murmured, 'I still want you.' His smile still took up half of his face. When he offered her a lift home, she agreed.

Nothing had changed there either. He pulled into the same gateway he had pulled into twenty years before, beside a brimming lake with reeds whispering around the shallows. Afterwards she didn't hear from him, but she wasn't as hurt by that as she once had been. Her life wasn't there anymore.

One by one, other things made this clear. The children lost interest in Ireland as they grew up. Her brother married and came home to farm. His wife, a blonde Afrikaner woman, seemed strange at first but she turned out to be as capable as their mother had once been. Susan saw that her home was in London now. Accepting all that as natural, they passed on old family things for her to bring

## An Evening Prowl

back: a delicate china tea set wrapped in newspaper, a silver travelling clock, a dark little portrait of her great-grandmother. If she asked some question about those things, her mother gave their history at length. Her father raised his eyes slowly and said, 'Aren't you sorry you asked.' He was stooped now, but still carried her suitcase out to the car. Tommy still rapped his knuckles on the bonnet and called 'God bless!' As if emboldened by her visit to the pub, he said, 'How's that husband of yours? He never comes over now.'

'He's getting old.'

'Sure if he wasn't, nature wouldn't be doing her job.'

He wasn't home when she got in, and their children were at university now, away. The house was empty. She unpacked her case, and set out some more old family things. She no longer wondered where he was. He was probably with Ede. He'd come in late and move around downstairs, making a sandwich from something in the fridge, turning on the television and talking back to the News – 'What the hell's going on in China?' – as if everything was normal. There was something missing in him. Like her.

A summer evening in south London: there was nowhere like it. When he had gone with her to Ireland, he couldn't wait to get back. Over there they thought shell suits were still in fashion. It bored him out of his skull. A police car stopped at Ladbrokes and he imagined helping with their inquiries: 'West Indian, early twenties, dark glasses. Yes, officer, I remember him clearly.' Elbow out the Volvo window, he headed down to the A24.

This was how he liked it, out cruising on the road. It made everything different, like being abroad. Without it everything was background, as familiar as Susan's white moustache after drinking milk, as Ede's black breasts. Women were sticky, they drew you in. He needed to keep moving. He turned off at the A238.

She was dragging in fifth. He was giving up unleaded. You didn't get the same performance. Ice-cream van music – 'Greensleeves' – was still weaving through the dusky roads. He pulled in to the kerb by the cemetery park, turned off the engine, and heard a blackbird singing. There it was on a telephone line, clear-cut against the evening sky. He could see its throat ripple as it sang, deep, strong notes, as if the earth's muscles were rippling. It opened its wings as if to fly away but didn't, as if it couldn't detach itself from the black line. He got out suddenly and went into the park.

## An Evening Prowl

Stopping for a minute he looked across London, the great sheet of light. He stopped again to look down at an old tree's roots bulging under the tarmac path. He couldn't explain it, any more than he could stop walking across the park. There was a condom wrapper, *Strawberry Flavour*, on the grass. The trees were dark against taller ones of silver green that stood out against the darkening sky. He stood to watch them fade into each other. It turned cold. He felt a yielding warmth as he stepped into the shadows.

When she looked into his room next morning it was empty and the bed was still made. He had stayed out before, but always with some excuse. She rang his mobile in the evening, but he didn't reply. She rang Ede – it had come to that – but Ede hadn't seen him all week. Next day she called the police. She was at work when they rang back. A man of his description had been admitted to hospital the previous night. Someone walking a dog had found him, lying on his side, whimpering.

He shrank away in fear when she leaned over the bed. She didn't recognise him either, his face was so bruised and swollen out of shape. The doctor said he had a hairline fracture in his jaw, broken ribs and internal bleeding. His red Nike top, with his money, phone and keys, was gone. The car was missing.

When he came home at last he was afraid of being left alone. In the mornings he watched from the front window as she went out to work. If the bell rang, he cried 'Who is it?' through the frosted-glass front door. When she returned in the evenings he asked questions about her day and sat up with her at night, talking or watching TV. Even his voice had changed: it was squeaky, like a child's. He asked if he could sleep with her, but she said it was better for him to try to sleep alone. When the police asked him to the station, he said he couldn't face open spaces on his own. She called a taxi, and went with him. She had to manage.

They watched CCTV of two boys filling the Volvo at a motorway petrol station. One of them was wearing his Nike red top. When the detective asked had he been with someone, he said he hadn't. The detective asked had he ever been with boys. He said he hadn't, he didn't know what had happened. They watched the two boys jump into the Volvo and shoot down the motorway.

As they went home together he told it all over again: he had gone for a walk in the cemetery park, and suddenly the rest was a blank. He couldn't explain it. The taxi driver looked in the rear-view mirror, but she didn't care. She said, 'You were prowling around and you got mugged. And you'd do it again if you got the chance.' He shook his head and gripped her arm.

It was months before he began to go outside again. When she came home from work, he'd be picking up scraps of litter or chatting with a neighbour at the gate. Sometimes he sat on the back patio for hours. She asked if he remembered what had happened. He said he hadn't. She asked, 'What were you doing before it happened? You must remember that.' He said he had just been walking under some trees. Saying he wanted to run it past her first, he asked one day did she mind if he visited Ede. She didn't. He went slowly up the road like someone going to work, and came back early. If the children were home for the weekend, he helped about the kitchen, preparing their dinner.

Lying in bed at night she tried to understand how it had all begun, when or where she could have cut it off and said, 'No more.' The lines in her forehead knotted, she couldn't see what had guided her steps. What more natural match for her than him, someone from another island that Britain had left; a local type she could never have married at home, who needed to be managed, held in check, who broke out, broke everything; that nothing less would have done; that what Tommy had said was true, 'Isn't nature a great thing.'

Lying in bed, turning on his side, his back, he tried to go over what had happened in the cemetery park. He couldn't. It was too much. He couldn't see that only someone like her could have allowed him to walk towards his unspeakable fear and smash open his shell; that instinctively he had chosen someone who would allow him to grow; that now he was in another element.

She called through the open door, 'Go to sleep.'
'What?'
'I said, go to sleep.'
'I can't.'

Each wondered what would happen next. Each feared and hoped they would hear a creak on the landing floorboards as one stepped across to the other's room. He might get into bed beside her. She might get into bed beside him. And talk. About what? That she was going to take an allotment and grow vegetables herself? That he had something to say? That their children were English? They didn't know. Then they slept.

Wind tumbled a beer can down the road. A magpie woke and cackled. The small things would go on turning into other, bigger things.

# BROTHERS

Marcus was staying with his brother near the place where they had spent holidays long ago. They had caught perch in the lake and fed worms to the wren's *scaltáns*, free as birds themselves for two summer months. In the city they spread butter thick on the bread, but on the farm their uncle's startled laugh taught them to spread it thin. Brod the blacksmith shouted at the local boys and them if they touched things in his forge. They used to cry when their father came to bring them back to Dublin, where they were privileged boys again. They had a foot in two different doors.

Though his brother had retired to the country he would not visit that place of holidays. His quiet refusal said it was the vanished past, but that childhood was with them still. Together they were easy when Marcus came to stay: he having breakfast at the littered table, watching the endless TV; his brother, not dressed yet, studying the sports pages in an armchair.

'Who's this he is?'

His brother looked up. 'James Fox.'

'Was he in *The Servant*?'

'That's right. With Patricia Craig.'

'Are you still doing the pub quiz?'

'I don't bother anymore.' Those were words his brother often used. He switched to Channel 4 for the racing tips, and Marcus said, 'I'll drive over to do some work.'

'See you this evening. I'll make a stew.'

Out on the bright wet road he enjoyed the morning air of freedom, the small surprises that belonged to this rough land. A mare and her foal grazing on a ruined mote galloped out of sight as he drove past. Touched by a rainbow, a distant white bungalow turned suddenly violet and green. In half an hour he was at that other place.

He had planted a wood there when he was fifty, and now the trees were twenty-five years old. They were beautiful in spring as the leaves opened above the straight tall trunks of the good ones; but in winter when they were bare he noticed the stunted ones and the cankered tops of those with dieback. If he looked through family photos he saw a similar change, from the laughing child sitting on grass covered with daisies to the old man with a tight mouth and a double chin.

He had neglected the wood, thinking it would look after itself, but lately he returned there to work: chopping thick stalks of ivy that had grown up every tree, pulling them from the bark and tearing up their roots, hacking briars, peeling off damp green coats of moss until the tree stood clean in a circle of open clay. But that satisfying work did not settle his mind. Here, alone, away from his books, conversation with his wife, the familiar city streets, his thoughts sprang up like the briars. Sometimes he stood rigid, shocked by a memory of something he had once done, and he released his remorse in angry cuts of the machete. He thought of the woman who had talked with him the other day, of what he should have said to her but had not. He tried to understand why his life had been so reckless, if it had come from running wild here as a boy. He wondered if the gulf between this poor place and that privileged city life had unbalanced him. He said an Our Father, trying to rise beyond his mind, but today he could not enter its simplicity.

All the time he was working, and when his seventy-five-year-old arm asked him to stop he had cleaned two dozen trees. In his garden in the city a robin would have appeared, picking for worms in the opened ground; but this wood was not a place for robins – a hawk lived here now. And lately buzzards had arrived, frightening in the dusk when their broad, silent wings rose like shadows from branches. Deer would be next, the neighbours said; they were drawing closer as young people left, and small farms became Sitka plantations.

He rested for a while, licking blood from briar scrapes on his hands, admiring what he had done, looking back at the hundreds of trees he had cleaned that year, seeing the smaller number ahead. His phone rang – his daughter? – he snatched it from his pocket, but saw another name and let it ring out. Again he felt remorse, and this time released it in anger at the neighbour who had knocked his boundary fence, a great old bank of bilberries and moss. Sure it was falling down anyway, Pat had said.

When he had inherited this place he had tried to make something of it, but the work was too much, he lived in the city and didn't want to be tied down. He had sold the house with an acre to a retired English couple, who had done what he never could. Now it was like a photo from *Homes & Gardens*.

Robert was on a small red mower, roaring up and down the lawn he had made from the field of rushes, swinging round a hen run, a polytunnel, flowerbeds. Robert saw him, but did not stop or even greet him until he had finished. He turned off the engine, got down from the seat, cleaned slabs of wet grass from the tyres, then said a chirpy 'Hello!'

'Robert. That looks well.'

'Just giving it a once-over.'

He liked Robert, or at least liked what he had done. The ass with the putrid fetlocks, the dangerous piebald mare, the ashes and the empty bottles in the nettles were gone. All that had been natural, part of wild freedom to him as a boy. When he had visited as a man the worst part had been saying goodbye, seeing the dog booted out, the door pushed shut, the bare light bulb come on in the kitchen, his uncle's gaunt face at the window, alone for another night. Now he didn't feel anything when he saw the house, and for that he was grateful to Robert.

'Saw you working at the trees.'

'No sign of the sparrow hawk. Is he still there?'

'He's around. Got a chaffinch this morning. Our bird table is his breakfast bar.'

Robert's wife was at the kitchen window, but she didn't look up as they passed. Robert brought him into the polytunnel to see how the marrows had come on, showed him a timber stairs to the hens' high coop, and the utility room he had made from the ruined turf house. He had plans for what was left of the old cottage, a barbecue maybe. Marcus looked at where his father had been born and said, 'You're doing great work.'

'I take a break now and then. Here, have a look at this.' Robert led him into a garden shed, where a miniature railway was laid out on a table. He turned a switch, and a train ran through pretty fields painted on plaster. He turned the switch off and the train stopped at a station, where the porter waited with a barrow and the stationmaster held up a red flag. Marcus said, 'All change!' but Robert pointed out that it wasn't a junction.

His wife came from the kitchen with food for the hens. Like Robert she didn't stop until her job was done, when she said, 'Hello' and stayed to talk. Her face was anxious as she spoke about Brexit, that it couldn't come soon enough, that England, Ireland as well were being destroyed by a godless Europe, which had brought abortion and homosexuality. Marcus would not agree. He said England had legalised abortion and homosexuality a generation ago, with laws more liberal than Europe's. She looked confused as she went inside. Robert went with her, and after a bit he returned with six eggs from their hens.

'See what you think of these.'

'I'll like them, I know.'

Yes, he was grateful for all they had done; without them his uncle's house would be a ruin like others around. The townland was as silent as his wood: that was the big difference now. The sounds he remembered – men shouting, women calling, children crying or laughing, the screams of a pig being ringed – were gone. But as he drove away he saw a jeep and a string of cars outside a neighbour's bungalow. The old woman who lived there had died some months ago. He stopped to pay his respects.

The kitchen was crowded with her son and daughter, and the son's wife and grown children. Now he saw the other big difference: the confident openness that free education and prosperity had brought. The son was a guard, tall and handsome, suntanned like a film star. His son, even taller, in camouflage trousers, was an army cadet. The sister was a guard as well. So was the Alsatian staring in through the window, she said.

'How do you mean?'

'He's in the Dog Unit.'

They laughed and talked as they sat at the table, eating steak and chips, drinking beer. Marcus was seated and given a dish of pasta with a cool bottle of lager. The son rang a number and went outside.

'He's like a hen on a griddle.' His sister tilted her eyes.

'What's the matter?'

'We've a man coming to mow the hay.'

Her brother came back and stood over the table. 'He's on his way. He said he'll be here.'

'Will you relax.'

'The rain will be here as well.'

'Have you much to mow?' Marcus asked.

'Nine acres.'

'You have six helpers,' one daughter said.

She was a beautiful, dark-haired young woman. Marcus looked at her. 'Will you know what to do?'

'I'm just driving the tractor.'

'What do you do when you're not?'

'I'm at college.'

Her father winked. 'They wouldn't let me go on to third level, for fear I'd get up to mischief.'

'I'd say that didn't stop you,' his wife answered.

Marcus had known this place when life was narrow and hard, when they picked stones from the fields, knocked a fence to encourage someone like him to sell. He forgot it all in his happiness that those days were gone. Instead there was this daughter checking her phone and reading a text.

'Emer saw Prince Charles in London. She says he's very small.'

'I met him,' her father said. 'I was on duty the time he was fishing back in Connemara.'

'What was he like?'

'Well you never saw such clothes. You'd swear he'd slept in them.'

Marcus smiled. 'No more than my uncle.'

'Remember the mice running across the table? You wouldn't know it now. Robert made a great job.'

'His wife is all for Brexit. She thinks Europe is a den of vice.'

'Sure I know, but they're good neighbours. They did the shopping for Mammy, and mowed the lawn when she wasn't well.' Reminded of the meadows, the son went outside to phone once more.

Marcus listened to the others talk among themselves about friends in college, duty in the army and sun holidays abroad. The land was still important but they had other lives. The sister cleared the table and took the leftovers out to the guard dog. Her brother came in calling, 'He's here, hurry on!' He looked at his daughter. 'You're not going like that?'

'I've jeans in the car.' She stood, and the tall soldier followed.

'You're ready for battle,' Marcus said but they didn't smile. There was serious work to do. They were balanced, solid, not like him. The jeep and cars drove away.

As for his brother, he was smiling too much when Marcus returned. An old man was asleep in an armchair, his chin on his chest and a pipe on his lap. Marcus lowered his voice. 'Who's that?'

'Joe. We had a few in the pub.' His brother went to the cooker and lifted the lid of a dirty pot. 'I was a bit late putting on the stew.'

The kitchen was as littered as their uncle's had been, though with different stuff: books, betting slips, newspapers, clothes, ashtrays of cigarette butts on the table and chairs, an umbrella stamped *Nurofen*, old fishing rods. Marcus felt a sudden smothering despair. This was where that childhood freedom had led to: he hacking his way through a silent wood, his brother sitting with a drunk old man like their uncle. The two halves of their life had never joined; the difference had been too much. He couldn't stay in, he had to get out.

'I think I'll throw a line for an hour.'

'Do. The dinner will be ready then.'

His brother took the pipe gently from Joe's lap and put it on a chair. Marcus took some fishing gear and left – but felt another shock as a woman approaching turned aside and walked past. It was the woman he had talked with the other day. He watched her out of sight, then slowly went down to the river.

It was high and loud from recent rain, the dark heavy water breaking white against the rocks. Trees and bushes crowded along the bank, until further on there was a space where he could throw a line. But putting up the rod, fastening the reel, threading the line through the rings, he was thinking of that woman. She would have met his type before, absurd old men who wouldn't lie down, with smiles that promised what they could not give. He tied on a fly with a knot he remembered, drew line from the reel and held it loose in his hand to let out as he made a cast.

A wind was gathering the clouds together, and now he thought of those neighbours rushing to save the hay. They would save it, he knew; they were disciplined, solid. He thought of their daughter driving the tractor, and of his own daughter who had not rung. He drew more line from the reel and made a longer cast that the wind carried lightly across the river. But still he was thinking – of the trouble his reckless life had caused, the running wild, the coming home, repeating that childhood ... He felt a deep, powerful pull.

The fish did not show, there wasn't even a splash. The clouds had darkened so the water was almost black, moving fast with the flood, rippling like hide, streaked by foam rushing every way. He held the rod vertical, a rough way to play a fish, but this was a salmon – it was too strong to be anything else – that he could not lose. The reel screeched as line was stripped off, five yards, ten, cutting through the surface with a force that strained his wrist. Suddenly determined, now he didn't give a damn for guards or soldiers, marrows or model railways. The line slackened as the salmon changed course, rushing blindly towards him, fighting for its freedom against something it could not understand. He reeled in fast, the line was taut again but the fish would not rise; instead it bored down deeper, and then was still. He could feel the line vibrating as the current struck it. It was as if he had hooked the river.

A small horse with dirty feathered hooves grazed among tall thistles. There were shouts from the football field as a practice match ended. A couple holding hands walked along the other bank, indifferent to first drops of rain. If his brother was here he would know what to do next, but he no longer fished – that was part of the vanished past. He reeled in more line but the salmon did not yield. The rod bent double as he reeled in again. He didn't care if it snapped, he had to end this. At last the surface broke and the salmon's back appeared, dark as the water. He drew it into the shallows.

It was exhausted, lying on its heavy silver side, but when he put out the net it gave a desperate thrash, the line fell slack and the hook came loose. It lay there for a moment but as he reached out again it was carried away by the current, floating on its back, its white belly showing, then turning half upright. He ran along the bank, hoping to see it swim, but his view was blocked by the trees and bushes.

The rain was spilling now, he was shaking with anger and excitement, but when his phone rang he snatched it out. It wasn't his daughter, the voice was English: 'I want to apologise for the way I spoke earlier ...' It was Robert's wife.

'No, that's all right.'

'No, I shouldn't have said those things. If God makes people in a certain way, we have no right to criticise them. And if people are presented with certain problems, we must try to understand.'

'I shouldn't have spoken so sharply. It's complicated.'

'But we must try to be clear ...'

He held on to that thought as he went back to the house, but inside it soon slipped away. Joe had woken up, and another man had arrived, standing beside his brother, watching the Epsom Derby. The man snapped his fingers as a horse streaked past the post, then he turned to Marcus. 'You were fishing?'

'He's taken over from me.' His brother gave his smile.

Marcus wondered now if it was the other way round – that his brother had taken on what he never had, joined the two halves, bridged the gulf and made a full life in the country of their childhood. As if in confirmation, the door opened then and that woman left an *Irish Times* on the table.

'You're all here.' Her general greeting included Marcus, politely making clear that she saw him as just one of them.

'The lost and the lonely,' the man said. 'I'm off.'

'It's raining again.'

'Sure it is.' Joe stood up. 'We get the hind tit in the west.'

'Take the umbrella.'

'Nurofen. The very thing.'

When they were alone Marcus and his brother had the stew. He explained how he had lost the salmon, and his brother explained that you never bring the net to the fish, you bring the fish to the net. Marcus said that it might have lived but his brother said that, exhausted, it had probably died. In the fridge there were strawberries, which a neighbour had grown, and cream, of all things. They enjoyed them as they watched *Miss Marple* and tried to help each other follow the plot, silently sharing the misfortunes of their lives; peaceful together, with nothing clear except their brotherhood, imagined and real.

He stood outside for a few minutes before he went to bed. The rain had gone, leaving a smell of fresh earth in the air. Small bats skimmed above his head, changing course every second to pick up midges. A satellite passed over, a steady bright spot between the stars, and he tried again to say an Our Father, reaching for the spirit that held everything ... It was as impossible to fathom as his brother. He could hear his coughing and the river's heavy flow as he fell asleep.

When he left in the morning his brother came to the door to say goodbye and then went back inside and pushed the door shut, the very way their uncle had when they were brought back to the city, crying.

# THE BATHING PLACE

A man lurched onto the train and sat down slumped forwards, smoking a cigarette, saying to himself in a drunken slur, 'I never begged from anyone …' A woman further up the carriage said in a polite American voice, 'Sir, do you mind not smoking? I'm allergic to tobacco smoke.' As the man tried to quench the cigarette, someone said helpfully, 'You could throw it out the window,' but the man said, 'I'm not that rich,' and slumped lower, rubbed the cigarette on the floor and put what was left into his trouser pocket. Someone else laughed in a good-humoured way, and the man tried to sit up straight.

He was about forty, well built but overweight, with a big sweating face that looked lost and defeated. He was so drunk it was hard to make out what he was saying, but everyone paid attention except a young Chinese couple scrolling through their phones.

'I'm just out of prison ... that's all I have—' he pulled a handful of cigarette ends from his pocket. They were crushed and mixed with ash, but he put them back carefully. 'And I got this—' he opened a plastic bag on the floor that held a blue nylon sleeping bag.

An elderly man asked, 'Have you no home?'

'I have, but I'd only upset the mother. She's bad nerves.'

'And where will you go?'

'I'm going out to Bray, I used to know a man out there ...' He checked another plastic bag that bulged with cans of beer.

The train went through the suburbs, past back-garden walls, a cricket ground, and then it ran along the coast; but no one looked out at the gardens, the cricket or the sea going by – they were looking at the man talking. He had a daughter ... she had cystic fibrosis ... he had taken her to Disneyland once ... he had gone down a wrong road ... but he hadn't done what he had been put in prison for.

His voice was louder but no one seemed afraid; instead there was sympathy in their faces.

They could have been looking at a tree tossed by wind or waves driven onto a shore, feeling release from their own anger and confusion. When the train came to a station the elderly man stood up, thought of giving him money but remembered his 'I never begged from anyone' and just said, 'Good luck.' The man gripped his hand, saying, 'I'm John Paul ... after the Pope ...' The elderly man drew his hand free and got out, wiped sweat and ashes from his hand with a tissue that he put in a platform bin, then walked down the road to the bathing place.

The bathing place is crowded in summer when the sun is out, the sea begins to warm and a south breeze lifts the lifeguard's red-and-yellow flag. Some women wear sunglasses while they swim; others bob in groups and chat, often for half an hour. A young man's back mottled by dark tattoos is like a seal's when he surfaces. Half a dozen girls of thirteen or fourteen admire each other's bikinis, then run together down to the water's edge, cry and run away, laugh and run forwards again, holding each other's hands. Some boys out in the water call their names – Kitty ... Miriam ... Naoise.

A young woman with red skin and ginger hair who undresses behind the wall, an old woman whose thighs are like bubble wrap, a man with a belly that hangs down to his knees: they are just like the handsome ones when they strike out into the waves. Some working-class boys and girls leave a radio playing hit music by their clothes while they splash and push each other under. A very old man leans a crutch on the handrail and inches down the slip, but in the water he lies on his back and floats. We are all one in the sea.

That was the elderly man's reflection as he dried himself, wrung out his trunks, tied the towel about his waist and walked the warm flagstones. The towels like togas, the blue sky, the sun made him think that ancient Greece would have been like this – men walking up and down, discussing the right way to live; no women in those days of course.

The handsome, swarthy Welshman who used to close his eyes to the sun and say, 'This is what life is all about' has disappeared. The woman whose husband died fifty yards from shore has tied a new bunch of flowers to the handrail. Even in this bathing place you can't escape deeper thoughts.

Hospitals had been for others until a few years before, when a hernia operation, and another for his prostate, brought home the slow degradation of his body. Standing for a moment he imagined dropping dead, the life that had held him together floating up to the clouds, recycled like some sort of rain and falling into other lives. He wondered who or what he might return as. As a cormorant like the one cruising through a raft of seaweed? As a small silver eel like the one wriggling in its bill? As a herring gull like the one on the wall, watching everything with its cold yellow eyes? 'How's it going?' he said, 'Are you OK?' The gull cried and flew out across the sea.

When he went back to his place on the long stone bench, a woman was sitting beside his clothes. She didn't look up, so he sat without speaking and tuned in to the talk on his other side. The girls of thirteen or fourteen were back from their swim, calling to each other in private-school voices as they towelled themselves.

'Did you see him looking at you?'
'Who?'
'Hugo – the one with the tanned skin.'
'I can't see without my lenses.'
'He lives on my road.'
'It's not fair!'
'Kitty, can I borrow your comb?'

He tried to remember how all that had felt. He couldn't. It was youth, a cumulus cloud of unhappy mad happiness that had dissolved so completely he wondered if it had ever been. But listening to the girls' cries of laughter, he knew that now they were in that high cloud.

## The Bathing Place

There was a stir as the woman beside him reached into a bag, and he turned to talk. That was another pleasure of this bathing place: ten-minute conversations with people you would never meet again.

'Are you going in for a swim?'

'Not yet.'

'You should. The water's clearer when the tide is in.'

'I'm going to read.'

'Plenty of time for that in winter.' He smiled.

'Do you mind if I don't talk?' She said it simply, politely, and took a book from the bag.

'I'm sorry. Of course.'

His face warmed and he knew he was blushing – ridiculous in an elderly man. He couldn't leave now – that would suggest he felt rebuffed. He couldn't even dress – to fumble on his underclothes beside her would be embarrassing. When she reached again into her bag and took out reading glasses, he glanced sideways at her: middle-aged ... henna-dyed hair ... a soft face, but with an individual stamp. He looked again. It was like diving underwater and seeing the blurred seabed come slowly into focus. He recognised her. She opened her book and leaned back against the warm wall to read. He sat in his towel, looking at his flabby stomach seamed with old surgery scars.

He had been a teacher, an aspiring profession, but he had worked with the poor – he had found a simple way of turning the glove inside out. Listening to rough stories and resolving their problems had satisfied his spirit, his desire for something more. They had met at a weekend conference in a provincial hotel, where, after the papers and the minister's speech, he had chatted her up. Long ago he had been good at that. He remembered her whispers in bed, her young face shining in the dark, a church bell ringing midnight as they made love. When he had said it was the Angelus, she had blessed herself and laughed. The conference had continued next morning, he had returned her smiles during the day, but when she had tapped on his door that night, he had said he wanted to sleep. Never before or since had he seen such bewildered hurt. She had been like a bird flying into what seemed an open room, and hitting the window pane.

An ice-cream van playing its barrel organ music swung down the slope and parked. He didn't look up when she stood, then he watched her walk across the flagstones to join a queue of children. He was one of those educated people who know their faults and feel satisfied by such awareness, so he had soon forgotten her; but her look that night had remained. Now he was old it sometimes came into his mind, as clear as if he had seen it the other day, and it seemed like an image his past wrong-doings had made.

The girls of thirteen or fourteen were busy doing their hair. One of them – the one without her lenses, he guessed by her brimming eyes – gave him a hesitant smile. She shook her head until her long wet hair was loose, leaned to one side as she combed it straight, then she stepped over to his place.

'I couldn't help hearing your conversation.'
'What?'
'When that woman said she didn't want to talk.'
'She wanted to read.'
'I know, but I thought you handled it really well.'

He took in the grown-up concern, probably learnt from good parents, and the bare childish feet as she walked back to her friends. She made him think of the man who had been released from prison, who had talked about his daughter and held his hand, whose sweat he had wiped away. He had an eye always for omens, like the scatter of stars in the night sky, at first a dazzling confusion, the constellations taking shape if you stood to watch. Everything was asking him to do what was right. He pulled on his clothes and stayed.

The woman returned, holding a cone at arm's length, licking drips from its side as she sat down. 'It's melting already,' she said.

'Yes, you have to be quick.'

She ate the ice cream quickly, cupping a hand under the wafer cone when it began to leak, then licking her palm clean. He offered his towel but she said, 'It'll wash off in the sea.'

She undressed before him, and he saw she had her bathing costume on underneath. He searched her eyes, and saw as clearly that she did not recognise him. In a minute she'd be gone, in a few years he'd probably be dead; what was the use of reminding her of something that could only hurt again? But he wanted to make peace with his conscience, and he spoke.

'You don't remember me?'

She looked at him and shook her head. When he mentioned the hotel, then said his name, she repeated it slowly and nodded. He felt a tension being released as she stood and tied up her hair.

He said, 'I treated you very badly. You must have been very angry with me.'

'I didn't understand. I was very young.'

'I still feel ashamed when I think of it.'

'Oh a lot worse happened me since then.'

'I'm sorry. I've often wondered how you were.'

'I was away for a good while. In England.'
'Teaching?' He looked at the set of her soft face.
'I was.'

He saw her wedding finger was bare, and asked, 'Did you marry?'

'I didn't.'

'Why not?'

'No one ever asked me.' She said it as simply as she had said, 'Do you mind if I don't talk?' She smiled. 'Did you?'

'I did. I still am.'

'You look well on it.' She looked at his white trousers, the navy French pullover with buttons on the shoulder that his wife had given him.

He said quickly 'I was seeing someone else when I met you.' It was like Confession.

She just nodded again. 'We've all been lonely.'

Afraid she would leave, he went on without thinking. 'Are you?'

'I don't think so. I suppose that means I'm not. Why?'

'Sorry …'

'Don't keep saying that.' She smiled again. 'I'd like to have married, I suppose.'

He threw out a remark he had heard somewhere. 'There's not that much to marriage. Two weak people join up and become strong.'

'I'm sure you don't believe that.'

'No. I was never any good at being unfaithful.'

'That's good.'

He went on, too quickly again, 'I'm sure you had lots of suitors.'

She shook her head. 'A few fiascos.'

A silence came between them like a third person. He felt his neck glowing. He said, 'I know this sounds vain and crazy, but do you think I harmed your faith in men?'

She closed her eyes for a long minute, opened them and said, 'Nope.'

He laughed for the first time that day, fully, from his stomach up. A man going by glanced them a smile. Bubbles of life ran through his blood. He felt a filament glow between them, as if their meeting had connected a broken wire, and he asked suddenly, 'Would you like to meet some day?'

'Why?'

'Just to talk.'

'I don't mind.'

'I do. I want to.'

Giving his phone number seemed too forward. He said 'I come here to swim most afternoons.'

She nodded and moved away. He pointed to a ship heading towards the port, and said, 'Wait till it's passed. The wake can be dangerous.'

'I'll be grand.' She walked down the slip and swam in a slow breaststroke out among all the others until he could not tell which one of them was she.

He went to the bathing place in the next days, waiting to see her, then relieved when she was not there. He had been forgiven – he smiled as he thought of her 'Nope.' Watching the tide go out across the sand, he reflected that she had simply done what he had done, and left him behind. Then the sea came in and broke against the slip, and her forgiveness brought back that look of bewildered hurt.

September came, the lifeguards put away their red-and-yellow flag, the thirteen- or fourteen-year-old girls went back to school, the days shortened. He spent more time at home, talking with his wife, arguing, then making up like any old couple – in out, in out, like the sea tide wearing stones to sand, bringing each closer to the other.

# THE GRAVEYARD

While he waited to turn off the main road the traffic going by threw flashes of water across his car. He set the wipers faster but had to lean forwards to see his way up the hill, and to park by the graveyard wall. From there he could see across the townland through billowing white curtains of rain.

It was bordered on two sides by a river, on the third by a narrow swift stream, and on the fourth by a mearing ditch. There were low sandy hills in the middle and below them spring wells that seeped every way down to the river, the stream and the ditch. Sometimes at night when he couldn't sleep, he followed the windings of the narrow swift stream back to the bog it broke from. His thoughts still went back to that place, but he no longer returned; he just stopped if he were passing to visit the family grave.

When the rain eased he went in the gate, up the tarmac path and across to a plot of mown dandelions and dock leaves. The rose bush he had planted had been mown years ago, and this time he found that the yew trees had gone; all that was left of their dark-green spires were the pink tops of sawn trunks. If he complained, Health and Safety would be the answer, he knew, as it was when they laid tarmac on the path, and cut down the row of sycamores by the wall. They loved chainsaws.

Putting aside useless anger he read out as a prayer the names on the headstone. Once so eager to spread his wings and fly far away, now he felt only gratitude for the care his aunts, uncles and grandparents had given. Anger and affection – his feelings here were always the same.

The rain lifted, and in minutes he was standing under a blue sky dashed with white clouds. Two girls in school kilts walked up the path to a fresh grave, where they placed a bunch of flowers wrapped in cellophane and blessed themselves. One of their phones began to ring, and they hurried out the gate together, laughing. 'Good on you,' he said silently.

Next came a man as old as himself, who walked slowly among the plots, looking at each headstone. He passed the Travellers' marble monuments at the back, looked round and came up to Marcus.

'Great day now.'

'Great, thank God.'

He was a priest, looking for the grave of an old friend from the town who had been with him in Maynooth. Marcus had been just a summer visitor and couldn't help, but enjoying the sun's warmth he stood listening to the priest's memories. His first parish had been in the Connemara Gaeltacht, though he had known little Irish.

'How did you manage?'

'I had to learn quickly.'

He talked about those poor days when each man put a single penny in the collection plate. To make some more there was a céilí every week in the church hall. He had once refused entry to a drunken young man, who had shouted, '*Tabhair as do coiléar agus tar amach!*'

Marcus smiled. 'So they weren't that afraid.'

'Indeed they weren't.'

He wore an electric-blue shirt that hung loose over brown slacks, the random lay clothes of a celibate. His white hair was centre-parted, his face was pale, anonymous. He was like someone

## The Graveyard

who'd had a nervous breakdown, Marcus felt, and been given a quiet parish by the bishop. He would have done his duty, said Mass every day, baptised, married and buried, living alone in a village presbytery. He walked away slowly, searching again for the grave of the priest he had known as a lad in Maynooth.

Marcus stood looking across the townland that was foreign to him now. An engine hummed in a water-treatment plant; loudspeaker announcements and grey clouds of steam carried from a factory beyond the river. But his memories of the poor fields were still there. The hawk with eyes like fire tearing open a small bird's breast. An evening dark with a coming storm when he had gathered mushrooms with his uncle. Bonfire night when a horse was jumped through the flames … Saying goodbye to the grave he saw a beer can among the mown weeds, and angrily threw it in a barrel.

The priest had given up his search and was walking to the gate, where they stopped to chat again. Marcus asked what would happen to the church, now vocations were dying out, but all the priest said was, 'God knows.' Irritated by his mild smile, Marcus asked did he know what happened when we died, but he simply said, 'I gave up trying to work that one out long ago.'

Across the road a JCB was clearing a slope, uprooting thorn bushes from a ditch with its claw. Marcus had not seen it when he had driven up in the rain, but now he remembered the family who had farmed there.

'Did you know Mattie Forkin? He was a priest.'

'Well I did. He was just a year ahead of me in Maynooth.'

'That's where he came from.' As Marcus pointed he saw the place was bare except for an old hay shed on the ridge. He felt as he did when a tooth fell out and his tongue touched the gap. 'The house was up there.'

The JCB rattled along the slope again, levelling the ditch bank, scattering its earth and scraw until the air brimmed with their pure smell and diesel smoke. 'And that's where Mattie came from …' The priest's face brightened. He remembered the last parish where Mattie had served, and the nursing home he had gone to, and the year of his death. The church had been his family, Marcus thought as he walked with him to his car. A woman wearing a black hijab sat in another car, looking or not looking at them through big sunglasses. The priest smiled at her anyway, shook hands with Marcus and said, 'It was nice to talk with you.'

'It was lovely to talk with you.' Marcus felt affection.

# The Graveyard

He tried to turn his car, but red bollards – Health and Safety again – narrowed the road below the JCB. To find a wider place he had to drive down the hill into that townland. A young woman out jogging passed without a glance. He passed what had been his aunt's house. The marshy field had become a neat housing estate where he stopped to turn, then suddenly changed his mind. His thoughts, the small events – the mown grave, the schoolgirls' laughter, his talk with the priest, the JCB – took him further down the road to a large bungalow. Someone he knew there was still living.

Going to the door he was nervous, hoping no one would be in, but then a boyish old man wearing a green baseball cap answered.

'You won't remember me—' Marcus began.

'I do.' The reply was quick. 'Marcus.'

'You have a great memory.'

'You had fair hair the last time I saw you.'

Luke's hair was still black and his laugh was still a cackle. As though Marcus was a neighbour who dropped in every day, he brought him through the house to a bright kitchen. In ten minutes they were sitting on high stools at a counter with two mugs of tea and a packet of biscuits; but Marcus was still nervous, making small talk.

'You have a fine house. Did you build it yourself?'

'I had to. The old place wasn't fit to live in.'

Marcus could see out the window a grass patch where the old house had stood. Its rough concrete floor, the chimney hooks and kettle thick with tarry soot had been a second home to him as a boy. It and others like it had opened his eyes to a wider view, that in time had given him a lot to sort out, a need that stimulated his mind as much as education had. He believed it had led him to be a writer, and his thanks had been to describe that boyhood in a book. His aunt had covered her copy with brown paper and hidden it in her bedroom. 'You made me out to be right dragon,' she had said. 'I didn't mind that. All I minded was you saying Luke's father hanged himself.' That was why he was nervous, keeping to small talk.

'What happened to Forkin's place?'

'The council bought it. They're going building social houses.'

'I remember my aunt sending me up to their house one night for milk. Mary Forkin gave me a full jug, but she never spoke a word.'

Luke nodded. 'She had a hard life.'

'I never heard that.'

'Sure old Forkin sent her home in her wedding dress when she didn't bring a dowry. She went to work in America, and came back with the money, and still they treated her like dirt.'

# The Graveyard

'Why?'

'She wasn't good enough for them.'

'They weren't that great.'

'They had twenty acres, the best farm in the village.'

'Did young Forkin not stand up for his wife?'

'He was afraid.'

'And did Mattie not say anything?'

'He went to Maynooth and he never came back. Oh you could write a book about all that went on in that house,' Luke added. 'No more than yourself.'

Marcus waited for the rebuke he feared. Indifferent to what others felt, he had set down his memories of this place he had loved, good and bad. But no rebuke came. Luke mentioned a woman in a nearby village who had also written a book. 'Oh an able cailín,' he said, and went on to talk of neighbours Marcus had known, the ones who had stayed in England and the ones who had come back.

'And the man who bought our old house, what's he like?'

'He's a yuppie. I'd hardly know him.'

Marcus smiled. 'You knew me.'

'But sure we were always close.'

Here, it had been natural that he visited Luke but Luke never visited him in the city, that he would go to college but Luke would go to work in England. It had left an empty space, a sense of something missing that he had tried to fill with his book, which Luke had surely read. 'It made out you were unhappy as a child, but you weren't,' his aunt had said. 'It must have killed you to write it,' she had conceded. In a way she was right. That was why he had not returned, but now he had come to face Luke, and been welcomed.

Relieved, he talked about shared days of their past: about the blue eel they had once caught in the narrow swift stream and given to a tinker, who had cut it in pieces – that even in the frying pan had twitched – and made a wristband from its skin.

'That was MacDonagh.' Luke took another biscuit, dipped it in tea and talked about a recent Traveller funeral, where white doves had been released and guards with guns stood outside the graveyard wall.

Marcus interrupted to talk about the time electricity came to the village, when Kate Caulfield couldn't turn off the light and tried to cut the cable with a scissors. Luke said her son had gone with him to England, and been best man at his wedding. Marcus interrupted again – his relief made him excited – and talked about his own marriage. Luke got in a word about life in England, saying it wasn't a fit place to rear children. Marcus told him about

## The Graveyard

his daughter, who lived with her partner in Dublin. Luke told him about his own daughter, who lived nearby with her partner.

'It's all partners now.'

'And no harm,' Marcus agreed.

They talked until evening, when Luke's wife came home. Marcus was introduced and welcomed in a warm Lancashire accent. She looked at the two mugs of tea and the biscuits. 'Is that all you gave him?'

'I was busy chatting.' Luke gave his cackle.

She asked Marcus to stay and have dinner with them, but he said it was late, that he had to get back to the city. Luke said, 'Call in the next time you're down, and we'll go for a drink.'

'You'll do that all right,' she answered.

'I will.'

They stood at the door together calling goodbye as Marcus drove away, but at the hill he stopped again, rolling down the window, breathing the air, going over what had happened. They had talked about everything except that damn book. Luke had not wanted to go over that past. He had knocked his old home of dreadful memory and built a new one.

The JCB had gone. Some rooks were busy picking in the open clay where Forkin's ditches had been; without the shelter of the bushes, the small birds kept away. A red western sky was glowing like raked embers through blue-grey clouds. Two girls with two boys carrying a bag of cans came up the hill from the town. One of the girls laughed when she saw him, and called, 'We're on the sesh!' as they went in the graveyard gate.

He remembered the night he had been sent up here for milk, Mary Forkin in the kitchen on her own, a row of copper dish covers hanging from small to big above a range, her silence as she gave him a full jug, the gripping wonder as he carried it down the road, under the sycamores in the dark, careful not to spill a drop. His visit to Luke had made no difference; he remembered the wonder as it was, and always would. He thought of it some nights when he couldn't sleep, the way he followed the windings of the narrow swift stream, still trying to grasp what it came from.

# A FAIRY TALE

Tom and Nicholas became friends when they were children, living on the same road and going to the same school. Nicholas lived in a secluded villa surrounded by a moat where goldfish swam among water lilies. Its white marble floors, the small safe set into a wall in the study, the maid in a white apron who gave him apple juice and Swiss yogurt had been like a fairy tale to Tom. He loved to visit there until Nicholas said gruffly, as if repeating something he had heard, 'I don't want you dropping over every day,' and Tom went down the winding avenue, back to his ordinary home.

They were brought together again by Barry, another boy in their class at school, whose father had died and whose mother could not manage. They discovered this one afternoon he asked them to his house, an ugly red brick mansion between a railway line and a river. Barry ran round the garden throwing stones, laughing savagely as he shattered panes of glass in a greenhouse while his mother watched helplessly, crying. When Nicholas invited him and Tom back to the villa, Barry was just the same, throwing an antique stool out the door into the garden, which he then explored. They followed him to an old stable and upstairs to a loft, where he had them roll up their sleeves, cut their arms with a penknife, press their arms together to share their blood and swear undying friendship. He was expelled soon after or his mother took him out, and he was sent away to boarding school.

By the time Tom and Nicholas went on to university they seldom met: without Barry their friendship was not so strong, and their different upbringings took them in different directions. Nicholas studied engineering, as his father owned an engineering firm. Tom's father had not been to university or even to secondary school, and respectfully allowed him to study what he chose. He studied English, not knowing what else to do, and over the next few years made other friends – 'seedy intellectuals', Nicholas called them.

He was with them one night in a pub near their college when a small nun came in. They looked up but she simply got change from the barman for a phone call, then left. Someone asked, 'Why are so many nuns small?' and Tom said, 'Maybe they walk on their knees?' His friends laughed and there were louder laughs from the next table, which flattered Tom. He turned and saw Nicholas among a dozen students, the college rugby team celebrating a win. They were both embarrassed by meeting, but when everyone stood outside at closing time they exchanged a few words.

'We're going to a nightclub if you want to come.' Nicholas was drunk, his round face was shining red.

'Let's go!' Tom's long ginger hair rose and fell as he jumped about, greeting everyone.

Nicholas went ahead with the team, who sang and stopped at alleyways to piss. Tom's friends did not come except for a boy studying German, who sang as they followed, *'Bist du bei mir, geh ich mit Freude.'*

'What does that mean?'

His friend translated it, Tom repeated it in German, then asked for the next line. He was quick and loved learning anything new. Nightclubs were new – he hadn't been to one before.

It was in a dark basement, where he danced to blasting music and shouted to girls he could barely hear or see. Hours later, sweating and excited, he searched for his friend but couldn't find him. A voice called, 'Tom!'

He called through the dark, 'Who's that?'

'Barry!'

When they went up the basement steps they found it was dawn. A blackbird was singing from a chimney pot, and they saw Nicholas getting sick into the gutter. Barry's blond hair was clipped short but otherwise he had the same wild, angry manner, crying, 'Nicholas!' and slapping him on the back to help him vomit more. Nicholas wiped his face, then gave a sudden smile: not his father's, or his mother's, but a blushing, shy, girlish one of his own that appeared sometimes for a moment like the sun through cloud. Tom danced from one foot to the other, to the music still ringing in his ears.

Barry cried, 'Where will we go? I've got a car!'

'Let's go down to the sea for a swim!'

'Fuck that!' Barry said they'd drive down to the docks and go to Liverpool for the day or the Isle of Man, but Nicholas said he couldn't – already he was going to his father's office in the afternoons. Barry seemed just as pleased to drive him home as anywhere else, speeding through the empty streets, crashing red lights. By then Nicholas was sober, saying in a matter-of-fact voice, 'Barry, what are you trying to prove?' and 'Barry, I don't know about you, but my life is important to me.' Barry drove faster, talking as he did sixty through the sleeping green suburbs. He had been expelled from the boarding school. He had inherited a share in the old man's pubs. The guy who owned the nightclub was a friend of his. Just mention his name and they'd get in any time. He dropped off Nicholas and dropped off Tom, then raced away in his open-top Volkswagen – his fist shot up to say goodbye, he swerved across the road to make a prowling fox run. Tom punched the air as well, not knowing he would never see him again.

Nicholas got his degree in engineering, then went abroad to do a business management course. Tom's degree in English was a shocking third class, but he also went abroad to study, still not knowing what else to do. He was in his boarding house one morning, trying to work on a paper, when the post brought a present from Nicholas – a novel called *The Third Policeman*, with a letter inside it. His handwriting was still big and round like a schoolboy's, making the news even harder to believe: he had got his business diploma, had met a girl, and they were going to marry. The novel was so frightening and funny that Tom read it all day, not bothering with the work his professor had set. At the end of the year he went home without any degree. Nicholas didn't ask him to the wedding, but he didn't care – they'd never had much in common anyway.

Tom's parents had come from the country, bringing with them some of their homely ways – on winter mornings his mother would bake a potato to warm his hands as he went to school. She had soon adopted the new ways of their suburb, giving her children sticks of raw celery for their teeth and calcium tablets for their bones. The school he had gone to was also new, and its priests treated the pupils like their firstborn: giving their free time to them after classes, teaching graceful tennis strokes, telling them the names of clouds and plants, explaining how a camera worked. Even snobbish Father Grenan had tried to help, explaining to them that it was vulgar to use a Windsor knot in one's tie. He had found Tom vulgar but years later when they met by chance and stopped to talk, he looked at him approvingly and said, 'You've changed.'

While other boys forgot their old school and lost touch with old friends, his school had been like a family, continuing to meet or falling out but still following each other's lives. Nicholas was a director of his father's firm, they heard. No one had seen or heard of Barry for years, except a rumour that he had sold his share in the family pubs and gone. They heard more about Tom, still trying to find a skin of his own, moving restlessly from job to job while his parents' tolerance went on stretching like elastic. He had thought of the priesthood, gone for an interview, and been relieved when the rector said it wouldn't be wise. He had worked in a poor country school but couldn't keep discipline and had to leave. He had tried office work, then teaching again in a poor city school where the boys threw stones after him as he cycled home. His father had given him a small allowance, and the elastic stretched a little more.

'Oh you look old!' Nicholas said when he ran into him in a city bar one day. Not for the first time Tom wanted to say something sharp, but Nicholas had a gruff certainty he didn't like to cross. That could explain why he was a bore: listening to him talk about yachting, Tom could imagine what drowning would be like. But then Nicholas blushed like a girl and gave his sudden awkward smile, and Tom felt for a moment he was meeting his old friend again.

Nicholas still liked him but wished he'd drop his *I came from the poor* carry on, join in and enjoy life. He had once asked him to dinner but wasn't asked in return, which made him feel he failed some test. Now he tried once more – 'We're having some friends in this evening if you'd like to come.' Tom's life was keeping all options open and he said 'OK,' then wished he hadn't, but felt he should.

When he saw the house, in a tall Georgian terrace looking over the sea, he changed his mind again. Through a neighbouring window he saw two tennis players on a wide-screen TV and stood watching, to delay. The window was open, the volume was up – he could hear the whop of the racquet, the grunt of the serve. He walked suddenly up to Nicholas' door and rang the bell.

It was answered by a boy, clearly Nicholas' son, who led him into a drawing room and silently gave him a glass of champagne. Nicholas came through the crowd, holding a cigar in one hand, touching elbows with the other, making introductions. He looked at Tom's casual clothes, touched another elbow, said, 'Patrick, do you know Tom?' then turned away to someone else. Tom had grown used to judging Nicholas and finding him wanting, so it was a jolt to find that now he was a small part of his world. Patrick seemed a bigger part, from his yellow silk bow tie to his shiny black patent shoes, to his smooth 'How do you do?'

'What do you do?' Tom tossed back his drink.

## A Fairy Tale

of his father's firm, they heard. No one had seen or heard of Barry for years, except a rumour that he had sold his share in the family pubs and gone. They heard more about Tom, still trying to find a skin of his own, moving restlessly from job to job while his parents' tolerance went on stretching like elastic. He had thought of the priesthood, gone for an interview, and been relieved when the rector said it wouldn't be wise. He had worked in a poor country school but couldn't keep discipline and had to leave. He had tried office work, then teaching again in a poor city school where the boys threw stones after him as he cycled home. His father had given him a small allowance, and the elastic stretched a little more.

'Oh you look old!' Nicholas said when he ran into him in a city bar one day. Not for the first time Tom wanted to say something sharp, but Nicholas had a gruff certainty he didn't like to cross. That could explain why he was a bore: listening to him talk about yachting, Tom could imagine what drowning would be like. But then Nicholas blushed like a girl and gave his sudden awkward smile, and Tom felt for a moment he was meeting his old friend again.

Nicholas still liked him but wished he'd drop his *I came from the poor* carry on, join in and enjoy life. He had once asked him to dinner but wasn't asked in return, which made him feel he failed some test. Now he tried once more – 'We're having some friends in this evening if you'd like to come.' Tom's life was keeping all options open and he said 'OK,' then wished he hadn't, but felt he should.

When he saw the house, in a tall Georgian terrace looking over the sea, he changed his mind again. Through a neighbouring window he saw two tennis players on a wide-screen TV and stood watching, to delay. The window was open, the volume was up – he could hear the whop of the racquet, the grunt of the serve. He walked suddenly up to Nicholas' door and rang the bell.

It was answered by a boy, clearly Nicholas' son, who led him into a drawing room and silently gave him a glass of champagne. Nicholas came through the crowd, holding a cigar in one hand, touching elbows with the other, making introductions. He looked at Tom's casual clothes, touched another elbow, said, 'Patrick, do you know Tom?' then turned away to someone else. Tom had grown used to judging Nicholas and finding him wanting, so it was a jolt to find that now he was a small part of his world. Patrick seemed a bigger part, from his yellow silk bow tie to his shiny black patent shoes, to his smooth 'How do you do?'

'What do you do?' Tom tossed back his drink.

'Property divilment.' Even Patrick's smile was smooth.

'Development?'

'Ten out of ten.'

'Knocking down and building up?'

'You can't have one without the other.'

'What have you been knocking down lately?' Tom was trembling as he said that.

Patrick gave a cold nod, went to get a drink and didn't come back. Tom drank another glass, saw someone he knew but didn't greet him. When Nicholas' wife came over, he said they had met once before, but he could tell she didn't remember. With a smile she asked what he did, and he said vainly, 'Nothing.' Looking round, as if for an interpreter, she beckoned Nicholas. He was drunk, Tom could tell by his red face, and his flat eyes that studied Tom's T-shirt.

His wife said, 'Is that some sort of statement?'

'No, it's a T-shirt.'

They didn't speak until Tom said he had to be going, when Nicholas said, 'You made a right pig of yourself this evening.'

Tom was hot with anger as he left: he wouldn't be seeing Nicholas again, not after that. He was glad: he wanted a life open to the world; full conversation, not drawing-room dialect. For people like Nicholas, thinking was like yachting or golf, something you did in your spare time. But he delayed again to watch the two tennis players still slugging it out on the neighbour's TV. It became a rally, both players crouched, swaying side to side, darting forwards and stepping back. One made a sly quick run and tipped the ball over the net, but the other got there and lobbed it down to the baseline. A cheer came through the window, a girl jumped up and punched the air. So did Tom, then he walked away.

It would be years before he saw Nicholas again, but news of him came on the family school suburb grapevine: he was drinking a lot … his son had gone to live on the other side of the world. There was even another rumour of Barry: that he had returned and was married. Tom had certainly got married, and Nicholas must have heard because he sent him a wedding present, an expensive sandwich toaster of stainless steel. Inside it was a card with the same schoolboy handwriting, *Call if you're out this way*. It sounded gruff, and Tom didn't call. He didn't want to slide back into that world of group assumptions.

His wife liked the toaster, and in winter so did he, when they took out a hot cheese sandwich scorched brown by the steel halves. It was made, he read in a newspaper, by a German company that

'Property divilment.' Even Patrick's smile was smooth.

'Development?'

'Ten out of ten.'

'Knocking down and building up?'

'You can't have one without the other.'

'What have you been knocking down lately?' Tom was trembling as he said that.

Patrick gave a cold nod, went to get a drink and didn't come back. Tom drank another glass, saw someone he knew but didn't greet him. When Nicholas' wife came over, he said they had met once before, but he could tell she didn't remember. With a smile she asked what he did, and he said vainly, 'Nothing.' Looking round, as if for an interpreter, she beckoned Nicholas. He was drunk, Tom could tell by his red face, and his flat eyes that studied Tom's T-shirt.

His wife said, 'Is that some sort of statement?'

'No, it's a T-shirt.'

They didn't speak until Tom said he had to be going, when Nicholas said, 'You made a right pig of yourself this evening.'

Tom was hot with anger as he left: he wouldn't be seeing Nicholas again, not after that. He was glad: he wanted a life open to the world; full conversation, not drawing-room dialect. For people like Nicholas, thinking was like yachting or golf, something you did in your spare time. But he delayed again to watch the two tennis players still slugging it out on the neighbour's TV. It became a rally, both players crouched, swaying side to side, darting forwards and stepping back. One made a sly quick run and tipped the ball over the net, but the other got there and lobbed it down to the baseline. A cheer came through the window, a girl jumped up and punched the air. So did Tom, then he walked away.

It would be years before he saw Nicholas again, but news of him came on the family school suburb grapevine: he was drinking a lot ... his son had gone to live on the other side of the world. There was even another rumour of Barry: that he had returned and was married. Tom had certainly got married, and Nicholas must have heard because he sent him a wedding present, an expensive sandwich toaster of stainless steel. Inside it was a card with the same schoolboy handwriting, *Call if you're out this way*. It sounded gruff, and Tom didn't call. He didn't want to slide back into that world of group assumptions.

His wife liked the toaster, and in winter so did he, when they took out a hot cheese sandwich scorched brown by the steel halves. It was made, he read in a newspaper, by a German company that

Nicholas had bought, and so he just sent a thank-you card.

'You should ask him to dinner,' his wife said.
'Then he'll ask me back.'
She said quietly, 'You're like a monk.'

As Nicholas had said, he looked old, but after a few years that stopped and his looks stayed the same. He put it down to marriage, and also to his work – his drifting life had led him to freelance journalism. In his forties he courted a newspaper with a series of sharp articles, which won him a staff post and condemned him to go on writing in the same way. He swam in summer, went running until one of his knees gave out, and on the long winter evenings he walked into the city for a drink.

If he had a local it was that old bar where he knew no one now, which suited him. He had done enough talking – that jar was full. The stained white aeroboard ceiling, the noise of conversation like a distant waterfall were reminders of the vertigo confusion excitement of his youth: buying a Chinese take-away at two in the morning, waking up on a canal bench without one of his shoes; that dark private party – 'Bite me. I said *bite*.' The taste of blood. Did he want that back? No thanks.

A grey-haired man strolled over from another bench. 'How's Tom?'

His journalism had made him a few enemies. He said carefully, 'Do I know you?'

'You do.' The wrinkled smiling face was like a Halloween mask, but Tom could place the nasal voice behind it.

'Hugh.' He had to move along the bench and make room. 'How's life?'

'Let's keep it simple.' Hugh gave a rueful shrug. 'What's the news?'

Tom knew what that meant, the only thing they had in common, the grapevine that went on spreading and embracing them whether they liked it or not. Like a knock-up before tennis, they exchanged a few remarks. Hugh enjoyed Tom's pieces in the paper – he said they made him laugh. Tom asked was he still practising law.

Hugh nodded. 'It's either boredom or danger.'

'Do you think so?'

'Ah yes. Fear's the only thing that keeps you alive. The unknown.'

'What keeps you alive?'

'Fear of the known,' Hugh replied.

He didn't trust Tom, who had written a waspish column about lawyers. Tom saw him as the sort who liked to seem immersed in life but kept his

## A Fairy Tale

distance from trouble; but he sat up when Hugh passed on the grapevine news. 'Did you hear that Barry died?'

'Barry? Who told you that?'

'Nicholas. He heard it from Jim. Remember Jim – in Foreign Affairs.'

'What happened?'

'A heart attack, he said.' Hugh paused like a raconteur before giving the punchline, 'At a cock fight in the Philippines.'

'A cock fight in the Philippines …' Tom repeated the words. 'He never changed.'

'I heard he was married. He must have got tired of that.'

'He hardly flew to the Philippines for a cock fight. Was he living out there?'

'Nicholas said he didn't like to ask. You know Nicholas, he's shy.'

'I never found that. How is he?'

'Not good. He's got cancer.'

'Nicholas has cancer?' Tom felt another shock.

'Drop in to see him while you still can.' Hugh raised his glass. 'Here's to Barry, he got out quickly.'

Hugh had his own troubles, but his mentioning wild Barry and dull Nicholas in the same breath irritated Tom. He said, 'Barry was different. He tried to live.'

'Did he? I'd say he was disturbed.' Like a lawyer producing evidence, Hugh went on. 'I remember a photo fell out of his pocket one day he was running around in school. When I picked it up and gave it to him, he said it was of his father.'

'You're saying the wildness came from his father's death?'

'Some of it,' Hugh qualified.

'And some of it came from the way we were reared.' Tom wouldn't give in.

'Maybe we were confined, but that's a cop-out. If you really want to do something, you do it.'

'Did you?'

'I tried.' Hugh was an easy-going conservative but a few drinks could loosen his tongue. 'You like to be a bit wayward but you never really stepped off the straight and narrow.'

'True. Nothing so wild as being a solicitor.'

'Ah fuck off.' Hugh laughed, and when they were leaving he said, 'Give me a ring some night, we'll have another drink.'

'Sure.' Tom didn't ask for his number. Hugh's face had a hurt, angry look.

Tom heard as much as he wanted from the old grapevine, but when it spread the news that Nicholas was dying he went out to the Georgian terrace by the sea. He wanted to make peace with their past. A woman answered the door bell, sized him up with a glance, then said Nicholas had moved years ago to a house in the next road. It was a secluded villa behind electric gates that slid open when he pressed a button. As he walked up the avenue Nicholas came to the door, leaning on a cane.

'Tom ... Your hair is white.'

'Why wouldn't it.' Tom smiled and held out his hand but Nicholas stepped back, saying, 'Covid. I have to be careful.' He walked slowly through rooms of antique furniture and paintings to a garden at the back, where there was fresh air and they could keep their distance.

'Will you have tea?'

'Thanks. I will.'

While Nicholas went inside, Tom looked at the garden, wondering what could they talk about, what was he going to say. Marble busts on pedestals stood along gravel paths; trimmed Virginia creeper hung like a curtain at the end. It was as formal as the house.

'You're younger than me, would you take this?' Nicholas came out unsteadily, carrying a tray in one hand.

Tom understood his embarrassment, and set the tray on a table. Nicholas sat down, stood his cane between his knees, then called, 'Do you want to join us?'

'Not yet.' His wife rose behind a tall bank of flowers. 'I want to finish this.' She waved briskly with a trowel, and bent out of sight again.

Like someone voicing a familiar thought, Nicholas said to Tom, 'It's not natural to live with the same person for fifty years.'

This wasn't the dull Nicholas who bored him, and he replied as openly, 'Goethe said it was unnatural, but it was the basis of civilisation.'

'Did he?' Nicholas pushed the tray. 'Help yourself.'

Two mugs of tea and a plate of biscuits were all he had managed. Cancer had paled his face, but his voice still had its gruff certainty. 'I see you're still writing for that pinko paper.'

'Why do you read it?'

'Well there's not much else. I buy it on the way home from Mass.'

'You still go?'

'I can walk that far. How about you?'

'What?'

Nicholas turned to face him.' Are you still in the spirit?'

'Do I believe? It comes and goes like the sea tide.' And when Nicholas didn't comment, Tom went on as easily as he could, 'Can you still go sailing?'

'No, the yacht's gone.'

'How about the cigars?' Tom smiled again.

Nicholas said indifferently, 'They're gone too.'

There was a silence then, that Tom filled with talk from the baggage of memories they shared, that held them together and reminded him how far apart they had grown, or had always been. 'I remember your father walking past our house every morning to Mass.'

'The half-eight.'

'My father used to say he could set his watch by him.'

'Your father was nice. He used to come over to visit him some evenings.'

Tom remembered those visits that had not lasted long. Socially unsure, his father had felt rebuffed and consoled himself by saying 'He's a bore.' When Tom mentioned that now, the first time he ever had, Nicholas just nodded. 'My father wanted to be alone when he came home from work.'

This was a strange conversation: now Nicholas was saying something he had never mentioned before, 'I wanted to be a doctor.'

'You never told me that.'

'I cycled into college when I passed the Matric, and put my name down for medicine. When I told my father, he said No, I was going to do engineering and work for our firm.'

'Why did you?'

'He wasn't like yours. You got away with murder.'

'I did.' Tom didn't know what else to say.

'What was wrong with you anyway?' Nicholas was gruff again. 'Always getting your knickers in a twist about everything.'

'How do you mean?'

'You never gave anything a chance. Backing away from us all as if we had the plague.' He added, indifferently again, 'Actually I have.'

'Hugh was telling me. Is it bad?'

'They've taken out half my insides.' Nicholas looked away. 'Did you hear about Barry?'

'Poor Barry. I did.'

'Not so much of the poor Barry. His wife had a string of pubs.'

'I never heard that.'

'Because you never kept in touch.' The gruff certain voice again.

Tom reddened like a schoolboy. 'Do you remember the day he cut our arms with his penknife?'

Nicholas didn't remember that, or Barry smashing panes of glass in the greenhouse. Tom had been the observer, watching from a distance. Nicholas had been physical, playing rugby, sailing a yacht, working for the family firm, drinking too much; but here he was, trying to connect, asking Tom about his wife and his daughters. Tom tried as well, asking Nicholas about his son who had gone to the other side of the world. It felt like a graceful game of tennis, knocking the ball across the net, until Nicholas replied, 'He never came back.'

'Nicholas, I'm sorry. God, what happened?'

'Ah, Tom, don't, please ...' There was no awkward blushing, just the pale, thin face. Tom saw with love the Nicholas he had never known.

They had known nothing of national schools, the GAA, summers in the Gaeltacht, student work on building sites in England. Tom's friends, the seedy intellectuals, had taught him a harder language and helped him to grow. He felt at ease among them, though they often argued. His friendship with Nicholas went further back, back to childhood, before he was fully conscious. Nicholas' moated villa with white marble floors had been part of a fairy tale; and so had Barry, who had pressed their bleeding arms together. The fairy tale had vanished in their lives of obedience, searching and rebellion, but it mattered still. In a way, Tom felt, it had shaped them.

Nicholas was tired now or had nothing more to say. He called his wife again, and she came across the lawn to sit at their table. As she talked about gardening Nicholas suddenly spoke, 'Why don't we ring Hugh and ask him to drop over?'

Tom feared as suddenly where that would lead to: group assumptions, enclosed conversation, everything he had fled. A healthy scab had formed over that past but it wouldn't take much to tear open. He made some excuse, and Nicholas walked slowly with him through the house to the door. Tom tried to shake hands, but Nicholas stepped back and they both made clumsy apologies. Nicholas said, 'I'll let you out' and pressed a button. Tom said, 'I'll see you again,' and went down the avenue to the opening gates, knowing they would never meet again.

# MISTER POCK – FINALE

There were people in these streets, like anywhere, who were just holding on, battered by age, deprivation, loneliness, misfortune.

There was Anne, who had worked in the Bird's Custard factory. They said she once threw an electric fire at the parish priest. She wore a Cancer Day daffodil in her hair. Some nights she used to knock on my door and ask questions.

'Who's this founded Saint Pat's?'

'Jonathan Swift.'

'That's it. I just couldn't think of it.' She used to look at my eyes and say, 'I'm not too bad, am I?'

She wasn't as bad as Miss Keane, who cycled to the church ten times a day, even in stormy weather when she had to push the pedals down inch by inch. They said her father had been a doctor. Her fingers were stained by all the cigarettes she smoked. Martina in the shop said, 'She's a real spacer, she is,' and imitated Miss Keane's airy voice: 'I'll take these now, dear! And pay you again!' – waltzing out with a packet of Players Blue.

There was Eamon from the country, who pulled a trolley of scraps he scattered for pigeons. He was another who lived alone. He made a wooden box to catch the mice in his house, then took it up the street and set them free. But there were always more. To identify one he put red nail varnish on its toes, and was touched when he caught it again – 'They come home.'

There was even a dog, Brandy, an old terrier, who was out on a limb. If you called his name as he went by, he wagged his stubby tail but didn't stop. He would be going down to the bus stop. The drivers knew him, and allowed him on board. They said he used to get off at the terminus, have a walk and take a later bus home. Anne said he had Alzheimer's. Miss Keane kidnapped him once.

And there was an old writer, me, who said his was a job like any other but he didn't believe it. There was something twisted about it.

All that could explain why Mister Pock was accepted. No one knew how he got his name.

## Mister Pock – Finale

He was a feral cat who had hunted these streets for years. You saw a shadow spring, a burst of feathers, and another bird lost its head. You heard kittens he had fathered mewing for food; bluebottle maggots once ate an abandoned litter alive. He was tamed somehow by Delia, a pious old woman, and taken in, but when she died he was back on the street. He had been softened by home comfort, and now he too was old. You saw him crawl on his belly towards one of Eamon's pigeon friends, looking stupid when it just stepped aside, not bothered to fly away. Neighbours left milk for him on their doorsteps but in winter nights he must have suffered from the cold. Then two young women moved into a flat around the corner. He had the luck of the devil always.

They were Indonesian, chambermaids in a hotel. Both were small, with names that were hard to remember, and so everyone simply called them 'the two girls'. They worked as a pair, saying it was safer that way; even on their free days they walked together. You never saw them with anyone else, which may have been why they took to Mister Pock, or he took to them. Soon he was rubbing his side against their legs, purring as he had with Delia, insinuating himself.

They began to bring him meals when they came home from work: grilled chicken, organic, with rice was his favourite. He was like that type who doesn't bother to look at the waitress. He ate and left. They worked long hours when they could; it was usually dark when they fed him – that was how they saw he had nowhere to sleep. They were paid the minimum wage and were saving to buy a house, but they bought a wooden hutch from the Camden Street pet shop. A neighbour allowed them put it in his front garden, and now Mister Pock had a home of his own, an impossible dream for them. The years slipped from him, you hardly noticed the grey in his sleek black coat. He was the young tom again, slouching around Harriet, the pussy in Number 50, warning rivals off his turf. Andrew called him Catanova.

The street was changing as people like Andrew moved in. He was an actor who kept hours as late as the two girls did, chatting with them when they visited Mister Pock. 'If I were a cat, would you look after me?' was one of his lines, but they didn't get his sort of humour. They were watchful, serious. One night when a guard went by they looked at the ground, and when Andrew laughed they whispered, 'Never laugh at the police.' They filled Mister Pock's bowl with Glenisk milk, and changed his bedding. If it snowed they put a plastic heater into his straw. 'It's called Snuggles,' they explained. When Andrew did a groan of desire, their embarrassment made him seem coarse.

He was acting, but there was purpose in everything they did. They did yoga meditation on Friday, so their minds would be clear when they chose the Lotto numbers. They said Moslems were kind to cats in honour of Mahomet, who had kept one as a pet. They went back to Indonesia, for a holiday, we thought, but they returned after a few days: they had gone to collect a legacy, smuggling out the money in their 'private clothes'. They didn't trust banks. Once when marauders attacked their village, they had hidden in a lake, crouched underwater, breathing through reed straws. We heard these stories while they tended to Mister Pock. His hutch became a meeting place where people talked when summer came: those warm nights of open windows, pale moths fluttering about the lamp post, the scent of buddleia that grew from the derelict garage.

Anne didn't need to call to me for company any more. I could forget writing for a while. Miss Keane had somewhere besides the church to visit: it was like a party when she brought fairy cakes to share. Andrew charmed everyone with his wit, and the purr he did when Anne admired his beard. Even Brandy, the old terrier, stopped to look. We met new residents, young people who didn't go to Mass but gathered at Mister Pock's hutch. The two girls had done what no one else had managed, brought us all together. They learnt our names, exchanged phone numbers, shoved gifts of food – vegetable samosa, chicken biryani – through our letter flaps. We told them about Mister Pock's wild past, and Delia's kindness. He had been faithful to her since she died – no one else dared touch him – but slowly the two girls won him over. He allowed them to stroke his head, caress his back, and one memorable night take him up in their arms. Everyone clapped. Purring, centre stage under the lamp post light, he made Andrew seem an amateur.

But all the time another character was circling this scene, Eamon the country bachelor. Word of his mice family had spread, and people complained of the scraps he scattered on the pavement. Now he found a centre for his good works in Mister Pock's varnished, felt-roofed home. Soon he was coming every day as faithfully as the two girls came at night. His food was poor, he had a stale smell, but step by step, from a touch to a caress, the same miracle was worked. By the end of the year Mister Pock allowed Eamon to hold him.

With his white bearded neck, his leather cap with furry ear flaps, toothless except for a few tobacco-stained fangs, Eamon had never attracted company;

but as he stood with Mister Pock in his arms, the neighbours stopped and chatted.

'He's looking well. How old is he now?'
'About twelve. That'd be eighty-four with us.'
'I hope we're like that at his age.'
'I nearly am!' Eamon could laugh.
'How's Andrew?'
'He's playing in the Olympia.'
'And the two girls?'
'Bono was in their hotel last night. The Four Seasons.'

Eamon was in the swim of life at last. Sometimes he stayed there for hours. He made a porch for the hutch, a trellis fence, even a doormat. Then, nuzzling his beard in Mister Pock's coat, he said goodbye, stood at the corner to wave, and went slowly home. Night came, the two girls appeared. A heated home, love and freedom, lunch and dinner – Mister Pock had it all.

He grew reckless, acting the teenager. One day he fell out of a tree and lay stunned on his back, giving terrible glimpses of what had been his manhood. He had fallen before, slept out in the frost, been cursed, survived poison, dodged stones and a pest warden's net – used up his nine lives. But what happened next was still a shock to us all: prowling the street, he was hit by a van.

The news spread fast. When Eamon and the two girls arrived he had crawled under a parked car. Confident of his trust, Eamon knelt down and tried to draw him out but the wild-cat instinct answered with a bite. Blood spurting from his hand, more hurt by the betrayal, Eamon went to have his wound dressed. The two girls coaxed out Mister Pock with whispers and brought him to the vet. His hind quarters were so damaged he would never walk again; the vet offered to put him down. The girls refused and brought him back to their flat.

He had lost what his double nature wanted, a home that was out of doors, but *he* was wanted, he still had that power. Miss Keane sent him a Get Well card. Not to be outdone Anne called with a tin of Whiskas, which he ignored. The two girls had his company, but the heart of Eamon's life was gone. He forgave the savage biting, the animal indifference to what others felt: he had to – they were part of what Mister Pock was. He wanted to win him back, but how? The girls were out at work all day, and at night never answered the door: like Mister Pock they had learnt not to trust the world. Eamon stood outside their window calling up, an old Romeo hoping for a glimpse of his beloved, but their curtains stayed shut. To show his care and assert his claim, he left scraps of food on their doorstep. The girls left them there. The fox from Iveagh Gardens soon discovered that.

When he called to me for help there was pain and anger in his voice, feelings he had never shown before. 'I've been shafted,' he said. He said Asian women were hard. He didn't believe they were afraid to answer the door at night; no, they wanted Mister Pock for themselves. Mister Pock was dear to him; he had known him long before the two girls blew in. When I agreed to mediate, he growled 'I want visiting rights.'

The first thing I noticed when I went to their flat was the double bed. They slept together, though not as lovers, I felt: I had never sensed that intimacy between them. They never showed a physical side, didn't wear lipstick or make-up, not even a ring or a necklace. They lived together like sisters, I guessed. But who can be sure of such things?

Whatever their love, it wasn't exclusive; to me it seemed out of control. Looking round the room I noticed other cats: a blind old tom, a lame tabby, a timid white one shivering on the window ledge, a delicate pedigree type they called Gracie and kept in a cage. Mister Pock had to share with these mediocrities now: that was price he had to pay for his care. He opened one green eye when I stroked him, gave a swipe of his paw – feeble, but it tore my skin – and fell back asleep. Did he dream of all his couplings and killings? Of kittens he had abandoned? Of the admirers who used to gather at his hutch? Or was he settling for a flat with two Moslem girls? Who knows what goes on in a cat's head.

They agreed to let Eamon visit, but it didn't work. He sat beside Mister Pock while the other cats looked on. What use was that? It was a sad duty, like a hospital visit. He watched the girls help Mister Pock to the litter tray, and afterwards wipe him clean with aloe vera toilet tissue. He had to accept that he couldn't give the care Mister Pock needed; worse, he had to accept that it wasn't what he wanted. He wanted Mister Pock as he had been: wild creature and soul comrade. Another feeling showed in his face – desolation.

He didn't visit again. Sometimes he stood beside Mister Pock's empty hutch, scattering scraps to pigeons, but the neighbours no longer gathered round; instead they asked him to move on. He turned in on himself, came out less often, grew careless. His chimney went on fire one night, and would have burned the house down if a neighbour had not noticed. When the firemen left, you could see through the open door what his life was like inside: old planks for imagined projects filled the hall. He was brought to hospital and discharged after a day; then the neighbours' talk returned to Mister Pock. A collection was made to pay the vet's bill. Andrew offered to do a charity show to pay for an old cats' home, but he laughed as he said it, and the two girls refused. He wasn't serious.

Passing their flat one morning, I saw its window was open, the timid white cat was missing from the ledge. The landlord said he had given them fair warning, they had left in the night, and no bloody loss. There were health and safety issues, the food left on the steps, the foxes; it would have been badgers next. Everyone was hurt that after all our years together they had not even said goodbye. When it came down to it, they saw us as outsiders.

I thought that was the end, but a year later one of them phoned. When I asked how they were, she whispered that they were behind with the rent, and had another vet bill to pay – could I help? I agreed, not from kindness so much as curiosity. She gave me their address.

It was a cottage half a mile away, the last in a poor cul-de-sac. A bush grew from the chimney, the gutter was hanging down. When I knocked, there were low voices, a movement of curtains, then they unlocked the door. Inside was their family of rescued cats that they introduced to me again. Gracie, the special one, was still in a cage, and lying on a red blanket by their bed was Mister Pock; they said he slept all the time, though his eyes flickered when they spoke. While we waited for their landlord I passed on my news. Anne had gone back to her old lonely ways, knocking on doors at night. Miss Keane was walking down the street again, swinging a golf club. Someone had stolen Mister Pock's hutch. Eamon didn't come out much. Brandy had taken the bus one day and never returned. Though they listened with concern, I could see they had moved on.

The landlord arrived, a tough, smooth type with a massive wristwatch that he looked at as I counted out a thousand euro. The two girls showed another side, giving him dark looks and muttering threats – he would have bad karma, he was not a good man. When he had gone, they showed me a film on their phone of an Indonesian cats' home they funded: there were hundreds, their eyes reddened by camera flash, mewing in a big dark room like a basement. I got out as soon as I could. When they phoned again, not to return my money but to ask for more, I refused. The next time I called, there was no answer.

It is three years now since they took away Mister Pock, but he could be alive still. Wild, tame, loving, cruel, he had learnt what the world is like and how to survive. He found his way into Delia's home of holy pictures and Knock water. He mourned her death, his loss of comfort, and found another home. He brought us together, broke Eamon's heart, grew too old for his double life. Now he is facing death somewhere far from the streets he knew. The two girls will give him that love they can't give to each other – for they have a higher love. At night from his red blanket he will hear them talk in bed. He will have learnt that they are serious. He will hear their whispers, then their sleeping breath as he is drawn slowly into a life beyond his own. You think something will go on forever, then it stops and becomes the past, a story.

# TWO COUSINS

He had slept for seven hours, a miracle, in a confused dream of a field he had known as a child: last night the field had been here in the city, his back garden the flooded corner where ducks foraged. He was woken by the clicking of their bills as they sieved watery mud, but it was his wife trying to turn her key in the front door lock. Still broken.

'Are you up?' She was back from Mass.

'Yes.' He worked his legs onto the floor. 'I'll get the paper.'

'Don't be delaying. I have a few things to do.'

'So have I!'

That was their marriage: a sudden disagreement that turned them into strangers, a silence as they passed on the stairs, some reminder of all they had deep in common.

Going down the street in the sun was the best time of his day, the morning hour when everything was fresh. A street-sweeper toothbrushed along the kerb. Women in cars did their make-up while the traffic stalled. Men in suits sailed to work on Dublin bikes. Yes, the hostel door was open, the homeless were being put out, but that couldn't keep down his thanks for being alive. A bagpipe skirl and drum *thump-thump* came from the barracks. He filled his chest with the martial air – Fáinne Geal an Lae.

Frank was setting out stock on the pavement before his antique junk shop: a life-sized plaster statue of St Patrick, a brass angel, a white marble holy water font.

'Where did you get this stuff?'

'That old convent round the corner closed down.'

'Who'll buy it?'

Frank patted the saint's green mitre. 'The laundrette put a deposit on himself.'

This was his quarter, where the strange was as natural as buying *The Irish Times* in Spar, scanning the death notices as he walked home. So many old friends had died that he was no longer shocked if he saw some familiar name. A memory of laughter, a row or perceptive remark brought a glimpse of them to mind, in the way the Dublin hills appeared and disappeared with twists of the streets. He waited at the corner for the lights to change, but a girl in school uniform swung her leg and pressed the pedestrian button with her toe. He took in the swing of her hips as she crossed the street, her air of youth's urgency, of future.

His dream of the field had been prompted – he was going down the country today. His wife said it was best to go early as rain was forecast. She laid out his phone charger and reminded him to bring his tablets. He asked her to stop fussing. She kissed him on the lips and he said sorry. She asked him to ring when he got there. Clouds were drifting across the sun when he set out, Raftery's song of home, *Anois teacht an earrach,* playing against his own thoughts, *Dublin and Mayo, the two wheel ruts of my life.*

After so many years he was used to it now: leaving the city, the rich farms of the Pale, cruising across the flat midlands, crossing the Shannon, then Roscommon's high slopes, passing stands of old beech trees, old demesne fields stretched between stone walls. The road went down slowly, the clear shapes unravelling in poor country that could shock him still. But after the shock another shape appeared sometimes – a sad patient freedom.

## Two Cousins

A length of new motorway took over, he greeted the Norman knight of shining metal on the embankment. Then came the Mayo county sign and he eased on the accelerator, ambling at forty, annoying a driver behind, who passed like a wind. Fast or slow, we all meet at the ford was his satisfied thought when they were stopped by a red hurdle. A notice said *Incident Ahead Diversion*, with an arrow pointing left to a byroad. He drew alongside the driver in front, a young woman, and called, 'What happened?'

'It could be a crash.' She had a local accent. 'Where are you going?'

He told her the village. 'Can I get there from here?'

'You'd want to know the road.'

'I don't.'

'You can follow me. I'm going that direction.'

She turned down the side road, driving in the middle, fast again in the country way, cutting through a flooded dip, going straight through crossroads. He slowed to look left and right, then had to drive faster to catch up – relieved when a tractor slowed her. She threw a cigarette end out the window, the tractor pulled into a field, then she put her foot down harder. Excited, frightened, he followed until at last she stopped on the edge of a familiar main road.

Drawing alongside again he called, 'Thanks!' and she called back 'No prablem!' Their eyes met for a moment – he took in her untidy black hair, open physical face, a lawless innocent look that made him want to stay and talk. But she drove straight across the main road, flashing her hazard lights to say goodbye, and vanished down another side road.

He had his bearings now: the petrol station, the closed-up national school, and a few miles further the side road that led into his own back road. A strip of moss along the middle, furze and withered rushes on either side – it was a lonely place but something was always happening. He glimpsed children through the bushes around Tarpey's derelict house, a quick wild handsome woman looking up from her phone as he passed.

A kestrel glided across the road before him, so close he could see a mouse with a long thin tail dangling from its claws. He slowed to watch it glide over rushes as brown as its wings into a hollow, out of sight. Jack appeared at the head of his boreen and glanced up the road. It was a year since they'd met, it would be rude not to stop, he wouldn't stay long. He drew in to the verge and got out.

Jack pulled the cord of a strimmer, cut a yard of briars snaking from the ditch and turned off the motor. 'She's working.'

'You have a lot to do.' Marcus looked down the long boreen to the cottage. The scaffolding was still on the gable – after what? ten years?

'Yess.' Jack's voice was precise.

'I often wondered why your house was built so far in.'

'The biteen of land they had then was in there. It was equal to them. They were far from everything. Walking meant nothing to them.'

'They say my grandfather used to walk the eight miles to the fair in Kiltimagh.'

'And thought nothing of it.' Jack undid a harness and laid the strimmer beside the ditch. He wanted to talk. He had begun at the head of his boreen, where he might meet someone going along the road.

It was an afternoon in early spring, the memory of winter fading slowly like the mountains pale blue in the distance. A few fields away some lapwings were mewing and tumbling in the air. A piebald horse whinnied, made a sudden run, then went on nosing in the rushes. A snipe flew in high circles above the bog, giving sharp cries as he rose and bleating as he dived. Otherwise it was so silent that Marcus could hear the bog water trickling down into the ditch.

Like almost everyone in the village they were related, but he had been reared in the city, was educated, married and travelled the world. Jack was the countryman who had never married or left his small farm. Those differences had been important: Marcus would roughen his accent and avoid fancy words in conversation; Jack would be shy, respectful. Years of casual meeting had worn all that away, and now they were simply cousins. They had the same slight build.

Two boys walked down the road, passing them without a glance or a word. Marcus said, 'Who are they?'

'They're after moving into Tarpey's. They're Travellers.'

'I saw them. I wondered who they were.'

Jack's eyes followed them. 'They say they don't speak to strangers, but I said hello to them the other day and they said hello.'

'It's better than having the house empty. Did anyone buy Andy's yet?'

'No, and they won't. Sure it's falling in.'

'And how's PJ? Does he still go to England?'

'He doesn't stay long any more. He leaves the electric blanket on while he's away. Oh the bottom's kicked out of this village entirely.'

'What'll happen when there's no one left?'

'We don't know.'

A bell's slow ring carried from Knock; Jack scribbled a sign of the cross and said a funeral must be coming in. The sun came out suddenly, brightening tiny tight hawthorn buds. A woman cycled by with a smile and a wave.

'She works down in the mushroom farm. She's Russian,' Jack explained.

'You know everyone.'

'She stopped to talk to me there last week. She said she can smell the sea from here.'

'But that's forty miles away.'

'It must be nothing to her. She comes from a place a thousand miles inland, she said.'

Where was better than here, Marcus thought, where wild swans grazed among cattle and a plane droned down to the airport? He was glad he had come. Swallows did the same, return to the first place printed on their mind. Absence and distance wiped out the boredom of wet days here, the stinking hen house, the horsefly and nettle stings, leaving a timeless image.

A car drew in to the verge, the driver rolled down the window, and Marcus saw the forester he had come to meet. Jack leaned against the bonnet, settling for another chat, clapping his hands on midges, saying they were a sign of rain, rubbing his palms clean and talking about the unnatural weather. He had been back in Lisglas the other day, helping to roof a house, and the sun had been so strong he'd had to come down. We'll be here till evening, Marcus thought, but the forester looked at his watch and said he had a few other places to visit.

Walking the patch of land that Marcus had planted, he explained what trees could be kept and what could be felled. He'd fill the forms for a thinning licence and send them to Marcus to sign. The larch weren't going to get any better; they'd do for chipboard now and something else planted in time. Marcus agreed without much interest – his little wood was growing into an endless business. When he left its shade and went back to his car, Jack's fields full of grey light were beautiful, and a hare sitting, ears erect, seemed at home there in a way it was not anywhere else.

Jack had given up strimming and was walking down the long boreen to his house. There had been no greeting or handshake when they met, nor when they parted, but that made their half-hour together all the more cousinly intimate. As he drove away he could see the rest of Jack's day: leaving the briars, as he had left the scaffolding, foddering the straggle of horses he kept as a sideline, making himself some dinner and going to the pub for a few pints: the bachelor small farmer whose way of life would not be changed.

That was how Marcus liked to think of it, something set and natural going on in the background, while he was leaving, refreshed, going back to his city life. But no more than Jack he had not changed either, and coming to the main road he thought of the young woman who had guided him there – her tossed black hair, open physical face, lawless innocent look, the flashing hazard lights. Slowing at the place where she had turned, he looked down the side road and wondered where she lived, what if they met again? All he saw, in the way he saw Jack's life, were glimpses of his own past: the innocence and cushioned freedom that had become hurt confusion, that had become assertive confidence, that had become indulgence, then dissipation – he pulled down a blind on their consequences. Putting his foot down again, he followed the main road.

A line of bare poplar trees like spears on a ridge, some green fields among forestry that caught the sun, a smoky edge of cloud touching a hill – they woke feelings that gave a bigger shape to his thoughts. Seeing a low signpost, *Tobar Naofa*, stuck in a hedge, he turned on impulse and drove down a narrow side road. It went through poor land like his own, planted here and there with a few acres of Sitka spruce, a stark new bungalow or two, but no sign of life. It ended in an open space where a stained old purple car was parked. Its petrol cap was missing – he thought of turning back, but hearing laughter he walked down a path and saw the well.

There was a low stone wall around it, and on a grass slope above it was a blue-and-white statue of the Virgin Mary. A teenage girl sat at the foot of the slope, a small boy laughed as he jumped from the slope onto the wall of the well. A tall young man stood awkwardly beside a woman who was kneeling – their mother, Marcus guessed. To put them at ease he reached into the well until he felt water, and blessed himself. The young man looked even more awkward then, but when Marcus smiled, he smiled shyly.

He was about twenty, with thin brown stubble on an unhealthy face. His sister sitting on the slope had long brown hair, lowered eyebrows that shadowed her eyelids, a hurt mouth, a defiant, helpless look. The small boy ran up the slope, laughing as he ran down and jumped again onto the wall of the well. Their mother went up the slope, took flowers from a bag and set them before the statue. She was heavy, out of shape, stumbling as she came back down the slope.

But she was the strong one and spoke without shyness. She said her name was Mary, then introduced her children: the young man was Martin, the girl was Theresa, and the small boy was Ted. They were Travellers, Marcus could tell from her

## Two Cousins

voice. He told them his name, Theresa asked where he was from, and when he said Dublin she began to sing – 'In Dublin's fair city where the girls are so pretty …' then she stopped and looked down at the grass. He had a shiver of delight for her harsh beauty, and of dread for what life might do to her.

'I reared them properly,' Mary said. 'There's evil in the world.' She rolled up her sleeve and showed the name Ted tattooed on her arm. 'That was my husband.'

'What happened?'

'He was murdered. Up in the North.'

'I'm sorry' was all Marcus could say.

'I think you're a good man.' She looked at him cautiously. 'Did you pray for your petitions?'

'I didn't.'

She took a tea light from her bag, lit it from a cigarette lighter, and set it among rosaries, coins and other offerings about the well. 'That's for your petitions.'

'Thanks. I'll pray for yours.'

'And say one for this fella.' She looked up at her tall son. 'I'm working to settle him down.'

'I'm sure he's a good son.'

'He can get mouldy from the drink. Can't you?'

He smiled less awkwardly but still didn't speak. As the others waited, Marcus saw that they were waiting for him to pray, and so he did. He prayed for them, his wife and daughters, and then for himself – asking to be single-minded, the same with everyone, to see that an honest life could not be dull. He felt peace breathe on him. In the same way he felt them watching from behind, all his desires felt part of a desire to be good.

Mary took up her bag and said it was time to go, but Ted wanted a last run down the slope and a jump onto the wall of the well. A stream surged from it, probably through an opening in the wall, but Mary pointed to it, saying 'That's a miracle.' She looked up at the sky and said 'When it stops raining and the sun comes out and you see a cloud, that's the gates of heaven opening.' Theresa said, 'It's not raining,' but she looked up at the sky.

What would become of them? Marcus wondered. They lived in an enclosed world that had no future, he thought as they walked with him back up the path. The young man got into the driver's seat of the stained purple car, and followed up the side road to the main road. When Marcus came to the motorway, he saw that they were still behind. Ten miles, twenty, thirty, and still they were following. He felt fright as their car suddenly drew alongside, but the young man just blew the horn, his mother, sister and small brother all waved, then they turned down a side road, out of sight. It struck Marcus that they had been pleased, grateful that someone like him had talked and prayed with them.

Looking in the mirror at the empty road behind, his life appeared as enclosed as theirs, as his patch of land, that dream place in the background where he had never lived, and today had wanted to leave after a few hours. As he drove back to the city, every fixed belief and clear idea scattered. All that was clear was the setting sun behind, shining through a split in slate blue cloud, throwing a beam across the country for miles ahead, covering bogs, fields and trees with an azure light.

It was later in the year, autumn, when he was away: in Paris, in an art museum, trying to look at paintings through a crowd. A girl stepped before him, and he admired her bare back's olive skin, her slight shoulder blades like folded wings; she seemed like a butterfly about to break from its chrysalis. As someone else pushed forwards he turned aside and went down stairs into an airy hall of white marble statues. A text came from a friend he was meeting, and he sent a reply. He was looking at a Cleopatra with an asp on her breast when his phone rang. Sitting on a ledge, he answered.

'In case you didn't hear, I thought I'd ring to tell you. Jack died yesterday.'

'What?' His voice rose. 'What happened?'

'You know that ditch by his boreen? It was flooded after all the rain we had. He was coming home in the dark, and he fell into it and drowned.'

An attendant wagged a finger, and Marcus whispered, 'I'm sorry, I can't speak now.'

'I know. You were cousins. Poor Jack, he could help everyone but himself.'

Going downstairs floor by floor he remembered their last meeting: Jack's wandering talk, the passers-by on the road. He wished he had stayed longer, been closer, but as always he had gone, wanting more. Now Jack had gone, drowned in that small place he had never left. Marcus felt a cold sadness. The streets could have been anywhere. He was glad to reach the café and see Magalie there.

They had met years before on a train, and spent the journey talking while her boyfriend was absorbed in his phone. They had exchanged numbers and met again in Paris, though her boyfriend had not come. Now she had left him, she announced. He drank and went out with other girls; she'd had enough of being a shadow. She was thinner, paler, her hair was veined with grey, she wore horn-rimmed glasses. Marcus said she looked like an intellectual Parisienne, but she reminded him that she came from a poor Normandy village. A boy there had loved her, but when she had gone to live in Paris he had married a local girl, and now she was alone.

She cried, then said, 'It's fair. I have to get a life of my own.'

There was a time when he might have wooed her with wise old-man talk, but now he spoke with conviction. 'It's not like that. You don't get a life. Life gets you.'

'How do you mean?'

'Life. It's what you're left with, after all the trying and failing. It's an emptiness really …'

'Oh don't say that!' She laughed, took off her glasses, then cried openly.

He tried to explain what he meant but couldn't; and she was too angry, upset to listen. They were like two cars approaching on a narrow road, neither giving way, a snap of wing mirrors as they passed. Silent then, they watched children dressed as ghosts and witches being spoiled by their parents. It was Halloween. The waitress wore a tricorn hat, a low-cut dress and a stuck-on moustache – she said she was Captain Morgan. Magalie kissed him twice as they parted, but he felt they wouldn't meet again. She was going to get a new life.

He was a believer in signs and portents, glimpses of a veiled greater world, a mystery that enclosed us all. That dream place in the background was coming closer, step by step, Jack's death turning it into part of everything. It was raining as he walked away, and he thought of the Traveller family praying at the holy well, his asking to be single-minded, the same with everyone, to see that an honest life could not be dull.

His phone rang, his wife's name came up. 'Did you get there?' she asked. Even through five hundred miles he felt an unearthly peace and cried, 'I'm here!'

A miracle.